IN THE SHADOW OF THE

IN THE SHADOW OF THE COMMANDER

David Dearle

The Book Guild Ltd
Sussex, England

The Book Guild Ltd
25 High Street,
Lewes, Sussex

First published 1997
© David Dearle 1997
Set in Times
Typesetting by Wordset
Hassocks, West Sussex

Printed in Great Britain by
Bookcraft (Bath) Ltd
Avon

A catalogue record for this book is
available from the British Library

ISBN 1 85776 154 5

CONTENTS

PREFACE

When my uncle died at the age of 90 in August 1982, he bequeathed to me most of his personal possessions. These included written records of his early life in the navy, spanning the years 1904 to 1920; some in the form of a diary or log, but the major part consisted of letters to his parents which somehow had been preserved and returned to him. Soon after he died I was contacted by the Imperial War Museum which was anxious to know whether he had possessed any records which would be of value to its archives. Since I had not at that stage begun to sort through all the extremely interesting material I declined the request. However, seven years later, upon my retirement, I myself approached the Imperial War Museum and showed them all that I had found. I had by then decided that I was going to gather everything together in order to produce a brief life of my uncle, with a special emphasis on his naval career at a particularly interesting period in history.

In 1989 I retired early from my post as headmaster of a preparatory school because I considered that my 16 years' tenure had been quite long enough. Nevertheless, I was under considerable pressure to explain how I would occupy myself after retirement. I had no doubts; all the same I thought that a good answer to all the questions was the one word 'research'. I would, in fact, research my uncle's life as a regular officer in the British Navy. The Imperial War Museum were most interested and helpful. As they were keen to add my uncle's material to their archives, I was perfectly happy to leave it with them on loan which no doubt will become permanent. They were good enough to photocopy it in its entirety for my benefit so that I could proceed with my research.

I have endeavoured to place my uncle's career within the context of his family. I have called it *In the Shadow of the Commander* because all the family of my own generation referred to him as 'the Commander'. He was a bachelor, somewhat distant, and we regarded him with awe, as indeed did his own brother and sisters. No one was more conservative than he, in every sense of that word. The Commander's approval or disapproval of any event that had taken place or was about to take place was definitely noted. As an undergraduate, on one occasion I hitchhiked down from Oxford to Dorset to pay a visit. The Commander quite definitely did not approve of that means of transport, and not only I myself but everybody else knew it. For all that, he was utterly reliable and in any family crisis he would do his utmost to help.

1

Eric Winthropp Woodruff was born on 7 December 1891, the fifth child and younger son of Dr John Winthropp Woodruff and Charlotte Louisa Jessie Shedden. I was myself the nephew of Eric, being the third and youngest son of his sister Aline Jessie. He was also my godfather. Eric had three sisters and one brother older than himself. There was a younger sister born two and a half years later. There were, therefore, six children in all. His father was a medical doctor, but although qualified (MRCS, LRCP and LM) seldom appeared to practise. He was my grandfather, and I can remember him quite well although I was never aware that he was a medical doctor until long after he died. He was born in 1850 and lived until he was 93; I was 12 when he died in 1943. It is true to say that most of the time I remember him as being in bed because at that time he simply took himself to bed for long periods. I never thought to question why. I probably thought that everybody did this when they reached a certain age. Anyhow, he somehow managed to get some long-suffering member of the family to wait on him, which was not easy at the end because of the war. His wife had died ten years earlier. My uncle Eric used to say that she was a saint, and the look on his face when he said this indicated that he thought she was a saint because she had to put up with his father. I think he must have been a difficult man to live with, if only because he was continually moving house. I believe all his six children were born in different places. However, they all lived to a considerable age. None of them died before 83, three of them reached 90, and my mother survived longest, matching her father at 93. My grandfather's mother had been a Winthropp and claimed kinship with John Winthropp, who sailed to America with the Pilgrim Fathers in 1620 and became the first Governor of Massachusetts.

The Woodruffs themselves came originally from Fordwich in Kent, the name having started as Woodreeve. My great-grandfather was Vicar of Upchurch, also in Kent. My grand-mother, however, was a Shedden and this family originated in Beith, Ayrshire.

I know little of my uncle Eric's very early years. Inevitably, as would have been the case with many children brought up in well-off Victorian households, he knew his nurse and his governess better than his parents. No doubt his mother was busy organising the household. His father seems to have been busy too. As I have already indicated, although he was a doctor, he had no patients, but much of his time seems to have been spent gallivanting round the country, locally by bicycle, further by train. Both my brother and I seem to have inherited this interest in railways. However, one could hardly have called my grandfather a railway buff. After all this was the only method of mechanical transport then.

From his diary for 1896, it appears he was frequently away for the day, sometimes for several days, travelling in all directions, ostensibly looking at future possible houses but very often because he just enjoyed travelling. For instance, on Saturday 6 June we read: *Went to London by 10.00 train: saw Peacock and Hardy about Practice. Lunched at Holborn Restaurant returned by 5.00 train.* At this time the family was living at Reading. On Sunday, 7 June, he stayed at home and went to church, but then on Monday he was off again: *Went by train to see a house at Beaconsfield, a nice garden but house not good enough. Went into the Church and saw the poet, Waller's, tomb in the churchyard.* He was home for the day on Tuesday but on Wednesday, 10 June, his travels started again: *to London and then to Southwold.* The following day he went to Cromer via Norwich, where he put up at the Red Lion. He left Cromer early on Friday for Tivethall, where he changed for Pulham St Mary in order to look at another house. He managed to hire a pony carriage to get him to Tivethall for the London train, and was home in Reading about 6 p.m., *Finding all well.* This remark appears frequently when he had been away for the night or more. Perhaps he did have a nagging conscience!

2

The first landmark in Eric's life appears to be his departure for prep school – Little Appley, in Ryde, on the Isle of Wight. By this time the family had moved to Binstead, near Ryde, and so Eric probably went there as a day pupil, although the 1897 prospectus shows that it certainly had boarding facilities. This prospectus has individual photographs of the outside frontage, dining hall, dormitory, library, a classroom, outer workshop, inner workshop, gymnasium and finally *At the end of the terrace*, with boys wearing Eton collars and riding or holding bicycles. It gives the impression that the school was quite progressive for its day. The foreword is written by Evelyn Rich, Surgeon to the Island County Hospital, and he testifies to the healthy, salubrious position of Little Appley. He goes on to say that the campus has been entirely free from all *zymotic diseases*, and testifies to the excellence of its sanitary arrangements. One would have thought that was taken for granted, but perhaps not, 90 years ago or more. There are also two school photos, sepia tone, for 1903. By 1903 it appears that Eric had passed the Oxford Preliminary Examination in Writing from Dictation, Religious Knowledge, History, Geography, Latin and French. For some unknown reason there is no mention of Mathematics.

In 1904 or 1905 Eric went to the Royal Naval College at Osborne. Who decided, or when it was decided, that Eric should follow a naval career I do not know. His elder brother, John Shedden, always known by his mother's family name, was now at Malvern College, from which he would proceed in due course to Trinity College, Cambridge.

No two brothers could have been more different than Shedden and Eric. Inevitably I am saying this from my own experience, and by the time I got to know them they were well into middle age. To put it bluntly Eric was very conscientious while Shedden was devil-may-care. Eric was also vastly more responsible. It never seemed that Shedden was a generation ahead of you. One example from later years was when I was at home during the school holidays (I had been teaching for a year, but was still very much of a bachelor and fancy-free). The phone rang one evening. It was Shedden, who said to me, 'What about going to Norwich this weekend?' I was delighted with the idea. I met him in

London the following morning. Norwich, as it turned out, was too far for us in the time available, so I suggested Chichester, an idea of which he thoroughly approved. We must have had something on our minds about cathedral cities, and we were off to Victoria station for the train. On arrival we booked in at the Dolphin and Anchor Hotel and went post-haste off to visit Westbourne, where he had lived for a time as a boy, and another example of Dr Woodruff's wanderlust. After that we returned to Chichester for a fish-and-chip high tea before finishing the evening at the cinema. Finally there was a nightcap at the hotel before bed. The following morning it was Matins in the cathedral before the return to London (via Portsmouth, for some reason), altogether a thoroughly enjoyable trip and all the more so for being spontaneous in the first place. However, I just could not imagine my uncle Eric initiating something of this nature. Plans had to be made for all expeditions and probably confirmed in writing before any move was made. Nor do I think that fish and chips at the caff was quite his mark either.

I am not sure exactly how long Eric was at Osborne. Cadets proceeded there from prep school at the normal leaving age and, I believe, spent two or three years there before going on to Dartmouth. In my own day (early 1940s), they went direct to Dartmouth from prep school. Also it appears that the Osborne training was temporary, existing only for a certain number of years as a step between prep school and Dartmouth. Osborne's one claim to fame is, I suppose, *The Winslow Boy*, and I have some vague recollection of my uncle telling me that this occurred during his time there. In fact, it must have been later, because it became news in 1912, the year of the *Titanic* disaster, by which time my uncle was commissioned sub-lieutenant. However, he would have been much interested in it at the time.

The next event he recorded was the training course for cadets in HMS *Cornwall* from September 1908 to March 1909. He would have been in his seventeenth year when this took place and everything points to the fact that it occurred when he was at Dartmouth. Some of the details of this cruise have been preserved through correspondence to his family, normally to his parents but on one occasion to his sister, Marjory, the second of his parents' children and nearly six and a half years older than himself. Marjory was actually her second name, her first being Frances. I never quite understand the policy of calling your child by its second, or indeed third name, but Dr Woodruff and his wife did so with three of their children. I have already mentioned John Shedden, who was always known as Shedden. The youngest of their children was Charlotte Alice May, and she was always known by her third name, May. She was actually born on 31 May 1894 so she only just qualified!

2

The six-month training cruise took the cadets to Halifax, Nova Scotia–Bermuda–Gibraltar–Algiers–Alexandria–Malta before finally returning to Devonport. Quite apart from its training value, there can have been few other situations where so many of the young can have had this opportunity of seeing so much of the world at one time. Nowadays, of course, it is quite different. Eric's first letter to his parents was dated 1 November and was from Halifax. Apart from the work, there is mention of recreation — going to the 'cinematograph' to get out of the rain, a football match against a local school. It's still very much school, with talk of half holidays. His comments about the local people are rather typical of a 16-year-old: *The people here get very annoyed if you call them Americans and their money foreign money. They are nothing but Americans, twang and all.* His next letter, dated 14 November, is from Bermuda and is written to Marjory, *as you say you have so few letters.* Poor Aunt Marjory, whom we all knew so well 30 or 40 years later, was always rather self-conscious and desperately anxious to be understood. *Please thank Father for the cheque for £2* – quite a lot of money in those days.

It is quite clear that what he appreciated more than anything else was the change of climate – plenty of bathing and picnics during their off time. Obviously there was plenty of work too. He mentions gun-laying, aiming practice, steering the picket boat. On one occasion, returning from Hamilton with the captain and some officers when it was pitch-dark, they missed the channel and ran into a coral reef and had to get help from a steam pinnace. He does not mention whether anyone got hauled over the coals for this, but perhaps he was not actually steering then.

He talks about being Midshipman of the Watch, but this must

6

have been a courtesy rank, rather like being NCO or Under Officer in the cadets, because they were all cadets and this was all part of their training. In fact, they became full midshipmen very soon after they returned in the spring of 1909. There is also an interesting reference to Boer Island, a small island where some Boer prisoners had been held during the Boer War, a few years earlier. Before he finishes this letter he mentions one he has received from his mother and also one from Aunt Constance (his mother's sister) enclosing a copy of *Our Boys Magazine* – I suspect a magazine with a somewhat religious slant.

This generation of Sheddens was somewhat evangelical, especially Aunt Constance. She was very sweet and used to live at Wootton House between Newport and Ryde. I can remember going over there for tea when we were on holiday at Sandown in the 1930s. She used to have a laugh which caused the young and uninitiated to laugh themselves. My brother once disgraced himself by imitating her laugh in her presence. My mother was, of course, mortified, but all was well because Aunt Constance was totally oblivious to the impertinence. 'Dear little fellow,' she said, 'laughing at all our jokes.' Progress was something that passed her by. Once when Shedden pointed up at an aeroplane, which during the first decade of the twentieth century was a fairly rare sight, Aunt Constance was ready with her comment, 'Don't look, dear. It's wicked!'

Eric's first remark in a letter of his to his sister Marjory is rather delightful: *I hope you will like this fairly long letter.* Eric makes mention in a postcard of a ship called the *Cumberland*, which had gone on active service over the Bulgarian question. Apparently in October 1908 Bulgaria's prince proclaimed independence, which was expected to cause a rumpus and upset the balance of power in the Balkans.

His next letter is dated 23 November (i.e. nine days later) and is written once again to his parents, this time from Bermuda. He first mentions coaling ship, which was noted in the last letter. By all accounts this was an extremely messy business. It is hardly surprising that frequently in ensuing accounts we hear how the ship had to be cleaned afterwards, and the cleaning took considerably longer than the coaling. It also seems to have been

7

on occasion quite a dangerous operation, because later on Eric recounts at least two fatalities during coaling. Other than this the letter tells of playing football, bathing and fishing. Then *Shopping in Hamilton, a funny little town but with a Cathedral.* He talks about catching squirrel fish and *school-masters* which have *stripes of all different colours on them.* Before finishing he recalls the arrival of an American gunboat, a term which would not be used much longer. However, at the end of the letter there is an intriguing postscript affecting the family: *Very surprised to hear of Shedden's sort of engagement.* What 'sort of', one wonders. *I will not tell May about it,* he adds. So, not a whiff of scandal to his youngest sister! However, it certainly did not come to anything because it was at least another 12 years before Shedden was married.

The following letter, dated 6 December, is again from Bermuda and sends Christmas and New Year greetings, but he then says rather plaintively that his Christmas and New Year will not be *merry and bright* because they are leaving Bermuda on 21 December and arriving at Gibraltar on New Year's Day. Obviously it was his first time away from home at Christmas. *Tomorrow, 7th December, is my birthday!* – his seventeenth. Obviously the letter was written over a period of about a week, because towards the end of it he refers to his birthday as having passed. Apparently the mail was brought up from New York on his birthday and he received his birthday letters on exactly the right date. Despite its being December it was very hot, and he says: *The bathing is delightful and the only way to keep you cool.* There is a postscript to this letter too: *Please keep all my letters for me as I want them when I come back.* Strangely enough, there is a further letter before they leave Bermuda, dated 13 December. The start is curious: *I hope you all had a good Christmas,* making you wonder whether he has put the wrong date, but he has not because he goes on, *I suppose Christmas will be over by the time this reaches you.* Also, he refers to leaving for Gib next Monday week, 21 December. He did not look forward to this because he anticipated as much as ten days of rough sea. He mentions earlier in another letter about suffering from seasickness. I gather that seasickness is not necessarily something you get used to and I understand that Nelson suffered from it throughout his career. Otherwise the letter centres round the officers' garden party with entertainment for the cadets. At the end of the letter he sends many happy returns of the day for 22 December to his sister Aline, my mother. She would have been exactly 20. Strangely enough there is another letter from Bermuda written the day before the *Cornwall* set off, i.e. 20 December. He says they set off across the Atlantic *tomorrow as soon as the mail arrives. We are going to go at fifteen knots and take eight days. Not looking forward to it much.* The ship had already been coaled. He had attended an at-home given by the Governor at Government House – *the dullest show* he had ever been to. *We did not know anyone and the tea was not very good.*

We hear from him again when he reached Gibraltar, although for some reason his letter is dated 3 December 1908. This must be a mistake and surely should be 3 January 1909 because he talks about the Christmas festivities and presents. In fact his opening remarks are all thanks for presents received. *Please thank Shedden for the little calendar. Aunt Alice sent me a very nice book bound in leather, called, 'Westwood Ho'.* Aunt Alice was married to Sir George Shedden, Eric's mother's brother, who had inherited Springhill in East Cowes, Isle of Wight, from his uncle; also the title Lord of the Manor of Hardmead, Buckinghamshire. He was knighted in 1926. Aunt Alice had been a Miss Gater before she married.

Eric's next mention of thanks is to Aunt Daisy for a postal order for five shillings (worth about 15 pounds in modern money). Daisy (actually Margaret) was married to Graham Eden Shedden, George's younger brother; she too had been a Miss Gater, and in fact was Alice's cousin. Aunt Daisy was something of a legend in the family. Her husband died in 1941 and she survived him by a few years. My brother remembers meeting her once during the war. She seems to have been somewhat twittery and rather delightfully unaware of situations. One anecdote tells how, at a children's tea party, in her endeavours to get the children to give due attention to the bread and butter before the rather more exciting cakes, she called out, 'Come along, come along, eat the bread and butter, dear little bread and butters!' She and

9

Graham had two sons, Harold and Eden. Harold for some reason developed a somewhat dubious reputation amongst the family; the suggestion was that he had over-sown his wild oats. Whether this was because he was married three times, as I understand it, I do not know.

Despite the five-shilling postal order, Eric was obviously short of money because he asked his parents for further funds for the rest of the cruise. But at last they set off. Initially it seems his fears were realised: *On Christmas Eve a gale was blowing and it was very rough, and we several times went gunwale under . . . I was a little sea-sick at first, but I soon got over it and towards the end I felt quite well.* Christmas Day itself consisted of turning out at 7 a.m., keeping their hammocks slung. After breakfast there was a short service, and then Christmas Dinner – cold turkey, plum pudding, fruit and nuts. The afternoon was spent in their hammocks because there was nothing doing and *it was warmest there.* It is hardly surprising that he describes it as the dullest and funniest Christmas he has ever spent – presumably funny-peculiar.

Eric recalls passing through the Azores and arriving in Gibraltar nine days after leaving Bermuda. *How glad I was once more to see land,* and then later, *We had tea in the town. It is quite English and has English money, but it is full of Spaniards and also Moors dressed in their strange garb!* They appear to have reached Gibraltar on a Thursday and during the next few days they had the opportunity of shopping in the town. He recalls how much of this was a matter of bargaining – the price conceivably starting at 15 shillings and going down to 2 shillings: *It's a funny way of shopping, so different from England.* On another day they went into the interior of the Rock and then another day out to the top of the Rock, from where they looked out over Algeciras to the west and, to the south, the Straits and, beyond, *the mountainous country of Africa.* He does not mention Sunday morning – obviously church as usual – but what is interesting, according to the HMS *Cornwall* magazine, is that Sir Edward Carson came aboard for the Sunday service. No doubt if it had been a few years later, Eric would have recorded it. However, it was not until 1911 that Carson became the spokesman for the Ulster Unionists and therefore a political figure of importance, although by this time he had already attained some prominence as a barrister by his defence of the Marquess of Queensberry in the first of the trials of Oscar Wilde.

At the end of this letter there is a slightly petulant comment to his parents, a little surprising: *You could have easily sent me a parcel as a lot of cadets had parcels and one had a large hamper with a Christmas dinner in it. A great many had Christmas cakes sent to them. Love to all at home. Your loving son Eric Woodruff.* Poor parents, how terribly we feel a bit of moral blackmail from our children. To give him his due, I think Eric was simply saying to his parents, 'We are allowed to receive parcels, you know.'

Eric's next letter is from Algiers and is dated 10 January 1908. This is clearly an error and should be 1909, a very easy mistake to make at this time of the year, although all our memories of Eric in the family were that he very seldom made that kind of error. Obviously there had been snow in England: *It's just my luck to be away.* The passage from Gibraltar to Algiers took about 36 hours. They arrived at 7.30 a.m. and it was very rough and pouring with rain. A 21-gun salute was fired for the French Admiral, but there was a delay in landing and they had not done so by the time he sent the letter off. However, his next letter is only four days later, 14 January 1909. Letters were apparently taking two days to get from England to North Africa. They had landed the previous Sunday after standing at anchor for 24 hours in the pouring rain. He was impressed by the size of the place, his original estimate before landing was that it was about the size of Torquay! I think he must have revised this because he now says that the population is about a quarter of a million. *It has electric trams. It's exactly like a French town, except you see numbers of Moors and Arabs.* The English chaplain took them round the Moorish quarter, in which he was most interested, especially watching the people at prayer. *It was such a contrast to European streets which are broad and clean.* Finally they took an electric tram to the other end of the town to see a rugby match against the French. Eric states that they were to leave on the following day for Alexandria and then Cairo. Mention of Cairo soon produces a request for more money. The original plan was to sail to Alexandria via

11

Syracuse but that was abandoned because of an earthquake there. According to the journal, HMS *Cornwall* reached Alexandria on Saturday, 16 January, and Eric's next letter is written on the illustrated notepaper of the Grand Continental Hotel in Cairo, and is dated 1 February. They had come up from Alexandria on a special train on 28 January. *The hotel is large and comfortable and the food is excellent.* He would be sorry to leave – hardly surprising after life at sea. Eric compares Cairo in size to Portsmouth and Southsea. They had a full tour of the Pyramids and the Sphinx – *No lady would be able to climb up or go inside as it is very slippery and difficult.* He himself was fairly tired after this and so in the evening he stayed in the hotel, although there was a dance at Shepherds Hotel. He did not go – *as I had no white waistcoat.* The following day they visited the Egyptian National Museum and in the afternoon they went to the ostrich farm and finally to the spot where Mary and Joseph were supposed to have halted on their flight into Egypt – not believed by the guide, *because he was a Protestant.* The following morning, Sunday, they attended the garrison church. According to the HMS *Cornwall* magazine this service was also attended by General Sir John Maxwell of the Yorkshire Regiment, just up from Alexandria. He was Commander of the British Army in Egypt from 1908–12, having served under Kitchener in the Sudanese War. However, he is best remembered for his part, in the aftermath of the Easter Rising in 1916 in Dublin, in the execution of the Republican 'martyrs', Pearce, Connolly etc., and he is known to the Irish as 'Bloody Maxwell'. The following day there was more sightseeing and he finishes this letter, *tomorrow we return to the ship.* He does not appear to be entirely sorry. *It is very tiresome!* (A very popular Woodruff word.) *When you walk in the streets you cannot walk in peace. Natives come up to you and worry you to buy cards and curios made in Birmingham, and to clean your boots. They follow you up the street and won't leave you alone.* It is a very long letter, and really one has to commend him for the regularity with which he wrote. Next stop was Malta.

The next correspondence is dated 17 February 1908 (he still cannot get it right!) from Malta. Apparently it took five days from Alexandria to Malta and it was rough for the last three. They found the Mediterranean fleet in the Grand Harbour so they anchored in Bighi Bay. He asks for more money to see him through the cruise, and speaks longingly of their coming return to England. *I find six months away from it quite long enough* and later, *looking forward immensely to coming home, it seems such a long time ago since I left with Aunt Daisy, Harold and Eden in the bus.*

Nothing much happened to him in Malta, apart from visiting a Dr Agius, a Maltese friend of Barnes, another cadet, and having to watch a match played before breakfast – starting at 6.15 a.m. He does not appear to be much impressed by Malta. At the end of the letter he says, obviously commenting on something in a letter from his parents, *Fancy Percy being ordered out here. I do not think it much of a place and I should think he would get very tired of it.* I would guess that Percy was Graham Percival Shedden, the youngest son of Sir George, who was born in 1886. He was killed in action in 1914, a regular soldier, which would explain his being 'ordered' to Malta. He was Eric's first cousin.

The final letter of the cruise is dated 3 March – Devonport and was *begun a long time ago.* He tells his parents about a tea party in Malta with his friend, Barnes, at Dr Agius's. Mrs Agius is mentioned as *quite like an English person, having fair hair, while all other Maltese have dark hair like Italians.* Then later he says, *Everyone here was very surprised to hear that I was seventeen, they thought I was only fourteen at the most.* In all the photographs one sees of Eric at the time he does look very young indeed.

They left on the Sunday for Gibraltar, where they did exams and he received a cheque with a letter from his parents, then set off for Plymouth on the following Saturday. It looked rough on Tuesday *in the Bay,* and they arrived home at Plymouth at 6.30 a.m. – *very cold with snow on the ground.* He came home on 18 March.

The next event would have been the final exams before being commissioned as Midshipman. His commission is dated 15 May, No. 258, and time gained on passing out is half a month.

3

From May 1909 to May 1912 Eric kept his *Journal and Notebook for the use of Junior Officers*, and this shows that during that time he was on the following ships:

a)	HMS *Implacable*	Battleship	15,000 tons
b)	HMS *Edward VII*	Battleship	16,500 tons
c)	HMS *Bellona*	Unarmoured Cruiser	3,350 tons
d)	HMS *Rattlesnake*	Torpedo Boat/Destroyer	938 tons
e)	HMS *Comet*	Torpedo Boat/Destroyer	747 tons
f)	HMS *Indomitable*	Armoured Cruiser	17,250 tons

This period of three years was presumably routine duty and one gets the impression that Eric is now the young adult rather than the schoolboy. He would have been between the ages of 18 and 21 during this period, and before the end of it he became Sub Lieutenant (April 1912). However, what is particularly interesting about this journal is some of the names mentioned. This is especially so, looking at it 80 years ahead – because it is often distance in time which makes for greater fame. Nor is there any suggestion of name-dropping on the part of an obviously impressionable young midshipman. They are simply brought in as part of the routine.

1)   12 June 1909   Prepared for inspection by Imperial Press Conference and Admiral Sir John Fisher.

Fisher was at this time First Sea Lord. He retired early the following year but was recalled in October 1914 as First Sea Lord in place of Prince Louis of Battenburg, but resigned again in 1915 over the Dardanelles Expedition. When he died in 1920 and was buried in Westminster Abbey, the crowds felt that they were mourning the greatest British sailor since Nelson. As a youth he had served in the Crimean War – in the Baltic – at the age of 14.

2)   *21 June 1909*   *The Commander-in-Chief of the Atlantic Fleet, Vice-Admiral* Prince Louis of Battenburg *came on board and inspected the guard.*

Prince Louis was treated very poorly because of his German origins and anglicised his name to Mountbatten, although I doubt whether this was the entire reason for his being replaced by Fisher in October 1914.

3)   *25 July 1909*   *At 5.30 p.m.* Monsieur Blériot *crossed the Channel in his Monoplane. Ordinary routine carried out.*

This was Blériot's famous cross-channel flight and the date given by Eric is absolutely correct. The recording of this feat seems quite matter of fact and the normal proprieties of the day were fully observed. Eric's ship was in Dover at the time and so that was why he was able to observe the event.

4)   *2 August 1909*   *8 a.m. Dressed ship, Royal Salute of twenty-one guns was fired as the Royal Yacht left Cowes at 11 a.m. to meet* The Czar. *At 3.25 p.m. manned the ship and saluted as the 'Victoria & Albert', the 'Standart' and 'Polar Star', with the two Russian cruisers passed down the lines. At 9 p.m. the fleet was illuminated.*

Who could have thought that within less than a decade Imperial Russia would be no more and the Czar butchered with his family at Ekaterinburg in Western Siberia? On this occasion, however, the Czar was welcomed to British waters by HMS *Indomitable*, HMS *Inflexible* and HMS *Invincible*.

5) 27 July 1910   *In the forenoon* HM the King *visited the various flagships of the fleet. At 10.25 a.m. he came on board us accompanied by* HRH the Duke of Connaught. *He left at 11.15 a.m. and proceeded to the 'Bellerephon' from where he went to the 'Dreadnought' where he hoisted his flag. At 3 p.m. the fleet weighed anchor and proceeded to sea in order to carry out tactical exercises before the king.*

George V had only been King since 6 May 1910 and the coronation did not take place until the following June. The Duke of Connaught, the King's uncle at this time, held the position of C.-in-C. Mediterranean. In the following year he became Governor-General of Canada.

6) 15 February 1912   *(Somewhere near Vigo, off the Spanish coast.) The P.Z. exercises that took place were conducted by* Rear-Admiral Terram *of the 'Duncan' and* Rear-Admiral Sturdee *of the 'Good Hope'.*

At this time Sturdee was Commander of the Second Cruiser Squadron. He made his name during the early stages of the war when, as C.-in-C. of the Atlantic and Pacific, and led the naval squadron which won the battle of the Falkland Islands (8 December 1914). He became Admiral of the Fleet in 1921 and died four years later (1859-1925).

7) 16 February 1912   *P.Z. exercises were carried out in the forenoon and afternoon. The*

> *Admirals conducting this were*
> Rear-Admiral Craddock *of 'HMS*
> *London' and* Rear-Admiral
> Maddan *of 'HMS St Vincent'.*

Craddock was also to be involved in a naval action in the early days of the war at Coronel in the South Pacific off the coast of Chile, on 1 November 1914. It was, in fact, a defeat, the *Good Hope* and *Monmouth* being sunk. The German force, under Von Spee, was superior in gunpower, speed and trained personnel. The cause of the British defeat can be traced to a faulty appreciation by the Admiralty of the whole situation of Craddock vis-à-vis Von Spee. The Battle of the Falkland Islands (mentioned above), fought in the same area just over a month later, avenged Coronel.

8) *26 March 1912*   *At 1.15 p.m. the 'Inflexible' came out and* Mr Winston Churchill, *the First Lord of the Admiralty and his staff came aboard us.*

This took place off Portland. Winston Churchill was 38 years old in 1912 and before becoming First Lord he had already been Home Secretary, both these posts being held in a Liberal Government, the last Liberal Government, in fact.

4

Eric's first ship after he became Sub Lieutenant (April 1912) was HMS *Ferret*, which, like *Comet* and *Rattlesnake*, was a torpedo boat/destroyer, but only 750 tons. He was with the *Ferret* until 1914, when he joined HMS *Nottingham*, a light cruiser, on 2 April. He was to be with this ship until 1916, and certainly it is the one of which he speaks with the greatest affection, and especially its captain, Captain Miller. It must have been very soon after joining that he took part in what was, so far, one of the most interesting experiences of his career, escorting the Royal Yacht *Alexandria* over to Calais for the visit of King George V and Queen Mary to President Poincaré of France. This was the 'Entente' tour reinforcing the original Entente Cordiale visit of Edward VII to President Loubet in 1903. It was a tremendous success.

My uncle obtained the *Daily Graphic* (price 1d) for 22 April 1914 and the *Daily Mirror* (price ¹/₂d) for 22 and 23 April. Both papers give full coverage of this visit. However, what is of particular interest is that Eric, having been in the escort party to Calais, where they anchored in the Calais Roads, was with a party of naval officers attending the review in Paris. Obviously the royal party had gone on ahead and they apparently detrained at the Bois de Boulogne station. Eric's party caught the 2.50 p.m. train from Calais and detrained as normal at the Gare du Nord at 6.30 p.m., the only stop on the way being Amiens. He was one of 12 officers and they were taken by motor car to their hotel.*We felt rather like Dukes driving through Paris in a beautiful motor car with a French sailor on the box*! They went to the Grand Hotel – *enormous and the best one in Paris*. He is equally impressed by his room, *with separate room for washing, adjoining. I feel more*

18

like a king. On their first evening they were taken out to a restaurant to dine. It was a magnificent dinner with an orchestra playing English selections. *It ended up with, 'God Save the King and the Mersaillaise* (sic)*, all the other diners in the restaurant cheering us*! After dinner they went to the Olympia and then on to another restaurant for supper.

They seem to have eaten well in those days. Nowadays you either have dinner or supper. They had both! Never mind, it was a festive occasion – splendid motor cars, illuminations, the streets thronged with cheering crowds. *So ended our first evening, on a most lavish scale,* and then in the next paragraph, *There are telephones all over the hotel and you simply lie in bed and telephone for what you want.* The following morning they had their breakfast in bed *in approved French style.* They all met up at 9.30 a.m. and there followed a tour of Paris by car, first to Montmartre and then to Napoleon's tomb in Les Invalides. After that they went through the Bois de Boulogne and back to the hotel via the Arc de Triomphe. *I had no idea that Paris was such a beautiful city and it knocks London into a cocked hat.* He describes the way chauffeurs drove their cars as being magnificent because they took no notice of the police. All I can say is that he most certainly would not have subscribed to that sentiment during the time I knew him – but then, of course, he was young, 22 to be exact. They had lunch at the hotel, a very good one but *really much too long.*

After lunch it was business, and they had to change for the review due to start at 3 p.m., wearing frock coats and swords. *We created quite a sensation in the hotel when we started in the cars at about 2.30 p.m.* However, time-keeping was not quite what it should have been, and since Eric was in a car which accidentally went a very long way round, and the traffic was so great, they did not arrive at the review ground at Vincennes until about 4 p.m., one hour after it had been due to commence. Nevertheless, he thoroughly enjoyed the drive, with people waving and cries of *Les marins Anglais*! On the way they had a good view of a large airship circling about overhead, and also about a dozen aeroplanes in the air at once.

They arrived at the review ground hot and dusty, with the

French officer in charge of them in a great state because they were so late, and they could not get to the seats in the stand which had been reserved for them. However, they were put in a gangway alongside the royal stand, from where they had an excellent view. Despite having missed the first half, he is quite sure they saw the better half. Companies of infantry and cavalry passed the saluting base with bands playing, and it finished with an attack by the infantry and then by the cavalry, which *was the best of all as they charged straight towards us amid the thunder of guns and maxims*. But the party had to move off sharply after all this as the gangway had to be left clear for the royal party. On the return journey they were just behind the royal procession. *We felt more like Royalty ourselves sitting up in the car with the people cheering us on each side, waving handkerchiefs and hats, and crying* 'Vive L'Angleterre' *and* 'Voila les marins Anglais'. As Eric rightly observed, *We had to bow back in answer*.

They eventually arrived back at their hotel at about 6 p.m. He then started to write a letter to his mother, but soon had to get into dress uniform for the opera. At 7.30 p.m. they were met at the hotel by the French officers dining them at their club, which was in the square opposite the opera house. The square was already filling up with people coming to see the royal couple driving to the opera. After an excellent dinner they went out onto the balcony to watch the crowds. *Here a most extraordinary sight met our gaze and one which you would never see in England. There must have been about a million packed into the square.* This last statement one does have to question. However, there must have been a dense mass, and both police and soldiers were trying to clear a space. This was being done *in a most brutal manner*; it sounds like flats of swords, batons and horsewhips. Troop reinforcements were coming up every minute, which could not have helped the density of the crowd. Anyhow, they started hitting out right and left, throwing people about. *The place was rent with cries. I wonder no-one was killed or trampled on by the horses of the mounted soldiers.* However, when Eric and his party walked across to the opera at 9.30 p.m., order had been more or less restored. They had quite a triumphal walk, being cheered all the way. *I came out with my hat raised like the King does.* The central stairway to the opera house was lined with cuirassiers with drawn swords.

They occupied two small boxes, where they had an excellent view of the royal box, but practically none of the stage. At 10 p.m., half an hour late, Queen Mary entered on the arm of Monsieur Poincaré, followed by King George V, who brought in Madame Poincaré. Sir Edward Grey, the Foreign Secretary, was sitting just behind the King. On their entry the orchestra played *God Save the King* and then the *Mersellaise* (sic); the whole audience stood up and faced the royal box. *The whole Opera House was crowded from top to bottom and I suppose it will be a sight I shall never see again.*

The opera consisted of three separate scenes taken from three modern French operas, the orchestra in each case being conducted by the composer. Eric did not think much of it, especially as he could not see the stage. They spent most of the time watching the audience, including the royal box, His observations are amusing. *The King, during the opera, looked very bored and tired. He kept putting his hand to his mouth in order to stop his yawns. The Queen was much better and had to prompt him all the time as to what to do.* By all accounts modern French opera was not one of George V's main interests!

After the opera, and the formal departure of all the dignitaries, Eric and his party went to a restaurant for supper, although they had already had dinner. He remarks that if in London they had gone into a restaurant in full dress uniform, it would have created quite a sensation but *not so in Paris, for they are so used to uniform that they take no notice* at all. They eventually arrived back at their hotel at 2 a.m. *thoroughly tired out.*

The following day was 23 April, St George's Day, so they all bought roses to wear in their buttonholes. They went to Versailles by car and walked through the grounds to the palace. They then went to St Germain *through the most delightful country and pretty woods.* At St Germain, where they arrived at noon, they had lunch in the old castle of Henry IV, on a veranda looking out on *the most magnificent view I have ever seen with the Seine in the foreground and in the distance, the Bois de Boulogne and the Eiffel Tower.* They left at 2 p.m. for a race meeting at Auteuil, attended by their majesties; no doubt this was very much more to George V's liking than French opera.

Eric's party was late arriving as their car had had a burst tyre, *the whole tyre coming off, so we were running on the rim for a short time.* However, they stopped for 15 minutes and got *the Stepney wheel in place.* At the race track there was a fashion show as well, which seems to have interested Eric more than the races. The royal party left after the fifth race, but Eric and his party did not leave until after the last race, reaching Paris around 6 p.m.

They were to leave by the 12.20 a.m. train in order to be in Calais and on board before the King and Queen arrived. After a final dress dinner at Coro's restaurant there was some sort of entertainment – *tango dancing and some singing.* Soon after 10 p.m. they left to finish packing and get to the station. They had reserved sleepers on the train. (There is certainly no such thing as a sleeper on the Paris to Calais train nowadays.) Eric slept all the way and they arrived at Calais at about 6.30 a.m., where a tug took them back to the ship. *So ended,* he says, *a most eventful trip. It was the finest time I have ever had in my life or am ever likely to get again. Everything was done on the most lavish scale and no expense was spared. I should think it must have cost the French Government between two and three hundred pounds.* Even for the days before inflation, I can only say it seems a most conservative estimate! Finally they escorted the Royal Yacht from Calais to Dover, then went straight off to Portland.

From Portland, after coaling, Eric says they would leave for Berehaven, in the West of Ireland to 'calibrate', after which they were to go to Lamlash to join the First Cruiser squadron. Shortly after this the letter finishes. However, comment is perhaps necessary regarding both these last two places mentioned. Berehaven in Bantry Bay is opposite the small Bere Isle. The narrow stretch of water between the island and the mainland made an excellent, albeit fairly small, naval base. It is now, of course, part of the Republic of Ireland, but it was to become one of the 'Treaty Ports'. The 'Treaty' was the Anglo-Irish Treaty of 1922, establishing the Irish Free State. However, one of the conditions was that, in the event of war, Britain was to retain certain ports, one of which was Berehaven. As it happened these were all handed over to Ireland by Britain in 1937, and were not available to Britain during the Second World War. There was, I believe, some bitterness about this because it was maintained that it would have made the naval struggle against German U-boats operating in the Atlantic considerably easier if Britain could have used the ports.

Lamlash is also interesting from an historical point of view. It is on the east coast of the Isle of Arran, in the Firth of Clyde, and has an association with the strained relations between Britain and Ireland at this time. At this stage, in 1914, the Irish Home Rule crisis was at its height. Ulster had made it perfectly clear that it was prepared to fight to avoid Home Rule. Ulster Protestants had the support of the Conservative Party, then in opposition to Mr Asquith's Liberal Government. Mr Asquith's First Lord of the Admiralty was Winston Churchill, and he it was who ordered the fleet, or part of it, to take up stations at Lamlash. Inevitably it was an action decried by the Conservative Opposition and Ulster Volunteers. Ironically, the Irish problem was solved, or rather postponed, albeit for less than two years, by the outbreak of the First World War.

However, before war commenced, Eric was on another engagement, and an equally interesting one. As a sub lieutenant on HMS *Nottingham*, he partook in the courtesy visit of part of the British fleet to its German equivalent at Kiel, very shortly before the outbreak of war. His first letter from Kiel is dated 24 June 1914, although he had started writing it in Weymouth six days before; *Weymouth, 18 June* is crossed out. The main part of this letter is, in fact, an account of his previous leave, which had finished up in Weymouth in time for him to join his ship. He obviously felt a little guilty about not having come home to see his parents, because the letter starts: *Dear Mother, I am so awfully sorry I did not come home this time, but I shall be getting plenty of leave next month before we go out to the Cape.* Because of the way the international situation developed during the following month, I doubt whether he had 'plenty of leave', and certainly he did not go out to the Cape.

5

The reason Eric did not go home on this leave was because he spent three days on a motor trip which he could not resist. He went with two other naval officers, Lieutenant Downes of HMS *Birmingham* and Lieutenant Crosbie of HMS *Southampton*. Eric and Downes went in Downes's two-seater Ford, while Crosbie went on his motorbike. The original intention was for them all to go on motorbikes but the luggage situation made this impossible. Having come off their ships at 11.30 a.m. on Sunday, they set off from Southampton at noon for Dorchester and Bridport, where they lunched. Soon after leaving Bridport the two in the car took the wrong turning at Charmouth, shortly after which the car *refused to go*. Eventually they ran the car down the hill into Lyme Regis in order to get some expert help. But the *help was not very expert*. It was now getting late and a thunderstorm was coming on. So they decided the answer to this was to have tea. Obviously it must have been the right thing to do because after their tea they managed to get the car going and left Lyme Regis *in the pouring rain*. Their worry now was that they had completely lost contact with Crosbie on the motorbike, so they continued through Axminster and Honiton to Moretonhampstead, where they arrived at 9 p.m. *just as it was getting dark*. It was nearly mid-June, but this was in the days before clocks were put forward or back. They had arranged to go on as far as Two Bridges, in the middle of Dartmoor, but in view of the fact it was getting dark, they decided not to go any further that night. They had somehow learned at Moretonhampstead that Crosbie had been through some hours before and had gone on to Two Bridges. So they spent the night at Moretonhampstead and poor Crosbie had to be on his own at Two Bridges, without his luggage! Apparently Eric and

Downes were being accompanied by Downes's wire-haired terrier named Felicity, *the life and soul of the party and the whole trip would have been a failure without him.* Presumably he meant 'her', unless there is such a thing as a male Felicity.

The next morning, Monday, was sunny and hot and they left Moretonhampstead at 8 a.m., arriving at Two Bridges an hour later, to find Crosbie perfectly well, but not yet up. After breakfasting and having a stroll up the Dart, they left at 11 a.m. – going across the moor to Tavistock and thence to Launceston, where they had lunch, but *as it was so hot this consisted of strawberries and cream only.* They continued on from Launceston to Boscastle, where they arrived about 3 p.m. There they discovered *to our horror and dismay* that they had dropped two of the bags and Eric's was the only one left. There was no boot to the car and all luggage had to be strapped on to a narrow platform at the back. Apparently bags dropping off was not unknown to them, but *we had always noticed before and had stopped to pick them up.* Fortunately they learned from a 'cleric' that a man had picked them up, put them in his cart and he would be in Boscastle about 5.30 p.m. So they went for a bathe at Bossing Cove, about three miles away, near Tintagel. They returned to Boscastle, where they had a walk up the Rocky Valley, and spent the night there. However, no mention is made of recovering their bags from the man with the cart. They must have done so, but the whole incident does show that, despite the advent of the internal-combustion engine, the horse-drawn cart was more frequent, there was far less traffic about, and greater certainty that incidents such as theft and vandalism just would not happen. We would not have that confidence today.

On the following day, Tuesday, they continued towards Newquay via Camelford and Wadebridge, where their lunch consisted of strawberries and cream, with the addition of cherries, which Eric describes as a *vegetarian dish*! Then it is on to St Columb Major and St Columb Minor, where they called at the post office to see if there was any answer to their request for the extension of leave for which they had asked. The answer was No, and so they had to be back by Wednesday night. Near St Columb Minor, at Portch Beach, they found a little private hotel where they got rooms for the night. What their sleeping arrangements had been for the previous two nights the account does not tell. They had a bathe in the sea and stayed in about half an hour *as the water was so beautifully warm.* This was the middle of June and I am surprised it was so warm but maybe it was well sheltered there. Later on, having bought provisions at St Columb, they cooked their own supper on the sand and had buttered eggs, mushrooms, bacon, bread and butter, washed down with cider; *Our cooking was a great success.* Certainly it makes my mouth water over 80 years later. They slept at the hotel and got up at 6 a.m. went down to the beach, where they made hot cups of Oxo, and then had another bathe, *a little colder in the early morning.* When they returned the tide had come in considerably, and they had to wade round the point with water up to their chests and holding their clothes above their heads. *This caused great amusement and we got very wet.* Fortunately, they had a change of clothes back at the hotel, where they had breakfast. They now had to start the 160 miles back to Weymouth.

They set off at 9.30 a.m. About three miles from Wadebridge something went wrong with the car, but it was only something that needed tightening up. The motorbike with Crosbie on it had reached Wadebridge, and Crosbie, tired of waiting, had told a man to tell them that he had gone on to Launceston. What amazes one now is that one could do this sort of thing and that the message actually would be passed on. The only trouble was that Crosbie *should* have gone on to Bodmin as Launceston was out of their way. Luckily, they met up with him, when he was filling up with petrol, before he had gone too far. So they were able to go on to Bodmin and from there to Liskeard and Tavistock. There they waited for about a quarter of an hour for the motorbike, but as there was no sign of it, they left word that they had gone to Two Bridges, where they had lunch at about 1.30 p.m. Then they continued to Moretonhampstead, arriving around 3 p.m.. Now they diverted four miles to Lustleigh, where Downes knew some people. They stayed there, having tea, for rather longer than they intended and did not leave until 4.30 p.m. However, they eventually reached Weymouth at 8.45 p.m. after a very successful run of 177 miles, *which shows what good cars Fords are for the money as they only cost £125 and he had already done 3000 miles in it including one run from Bristol to Newcastle.*

But what of Crosbie, the motorcyclist? He had apparently had a breakdown with a broken piston and had to come back by train. I hope he made it in time! Bodmin to Exeter should have been all right, but Exeter to Weymouth by train is a very difficult journey and always has been. As far as Eric was concerned, *It was quite one of the happiest leaves I have spent, and it only cost us about a pound each!*

6

After this interlude the content of the letter returned to the affairs of HMS *Nottingham*. They left for Kiel on Friday and encountered very thick fog until Saturday night. Some ships came so close that they could talk to them, although they could not see them. After the fog cleared they made better progress and they anchored on Monday night, about 12 miles from Kiel, and on Tuesday morning came into Kiel. The port was full of German warships. Their squadron consisted of four battleships – *King George V, Centurion, Ajax* and *Audacious* – and three cruisers – *Southampton, Birmingham* and *Nottingham*. This was a courtesy visit. *We have had a tremendous amount of invitations to various functions and there has been much interchange of visits between the ships. The 'Hohenzollern' with the Kaiser on board, arrived today and the ships were manned and salutes fired.* Everything was very formal. They were not allowed to go ashore except in uniform frock coats and *in consequence there is not much competition for the beach*! However, he was looking forward to going to Hamburg on Friday to see the zoo there because for that they do not need to wear uniform. Then there is a very direct comment: *We shall all be very glad to leave this place as the Germans are too critical and any little thing we do is published in the papers and sneering remarks made about it, which I think is very rude. We would not think of doing the same sort of thing in England, but the Germans have no manners at all. The reception we get here is very different to what we get from the French.* The Entente Cordiale seemed to be working!

In the next paragraph of the letter he talks about the regatta beginning the following day. He bemoans the fact that they were handicapped by only one officer being able to speak any German.

Luckily, he says, *all the German officers speak English like natives*. However, almost to offset this undoubted advantage to the other side, he says rather defensively, *I don't think their ships or men are so smart as ours*. He finishes this lengthy letter with a postscript in which he states there have been half a dozen aeroplanes flying about, but what fascinated him most was a Zeppelin.

When Eric writes again it is from Kiel on 28 June 1914, only four days after his previous letter. Enough was enough, it seemed: *We are getting very tired of Kiel and all its functions, as they don't leave us a minute's peace*. The previous Thursday they had been entertained to a grand luncheon on board the German cruiser *Mainz*, during which Eric met Phyllis Tipping, presumably a family friend, but what is of particular interest is that she was the guest of Admiral Von Coerper, with whom she was apparently staying. Eric talked to her, and while doing so Admiral Von Coerper came up with a British admiral and Eric was introduced and given a special invitation to a garden party and dance on the Sunday, *So I was all amongst the elite*. He is somewhat cynical, however, about Phyllis Tipping, who *seems to be having a very good time going to all the functions and will now hardly talk to anyone below an Admiral*. This was slightly harsh judgment in view of the fact she had at least spoken to one sub lieutenant!

The trip to Hamburg, mentioned in the last letter, came off. He went there with a fellow officer, Brooks, travelling on the 9.10 a.m. train from Kiel. It is a journey I have done myself by rail, when it took about 80 minutes. He describes Hamburg as an enormous place, and that was my impression too, in 1986. They managed to get to the zoo, although he experienced disappointment that it was not as good as he had been led to expect. They had the better part of a day in Hamburg and went back on board at about 11.30 p.m.

The following day he went to Admiral Von Coerper's garden party, *a thoroughly stiff affair*. In the evening there was a grand dinner aboard the *Nottingham* for the officer of the *Mainz* and *Stralsund* in return for their lunch party. The next three events sound like an exercise in name-dropping. Firstly, there is a garden party given by the Prince and Princess of Prussia, although Eric said that for some reason or other it was put off. Secondly, a dance was given by Admiral Von Coerper. I wonder what part he played in the war. Was he at Jutland? Thirdly, *The Kaiser passed close to the ship today in his yacht, the 'Meteor'*.

Despite all this excitement he looks forward to leaving, especially as there is a chance they may go via the Kiel Canal. Clearly he seems to be almost overwhelmed by the social round. *There are so many functions going on that one has to be practically in two places at once.* He had much sympathy with his captain, whom he describes as *not having much of a time as he leaves the ship generally after breakfast and does not return until 11.00 p.m., except just to change his clothes and go on to the next thing.*

The next letter* starts *Dear Father*, but he generally wrote to his mother, and seldom to both of them together. However, perhaps this was necessitated by his *thank you very much for the cheque.* This is dated 3 July 1914 and is from Immingham, the nearest port to Nottingham, where they were expected for festivities. They had left Kiel on a Tuesday morning and come through the Canal which had taken eight hours. *All day we were passing through pretty scenery of woods and fields and farm houses. It seemed so funny and out of place with the ship which one always associates with the sea. We had to strike our topmasts in order to get under the bridges.* However, it is the next paragraph in the letter which really stops you in your tracks, all the more so because of the comparatively casual way in which it is mentioned. *All the festivities arranged for on Sunday and Monday were put off owing to the assassination of the Crown Prince of Austria, so we had a welcome rest on those two days.* What meant a 'welcome rest' to Eric was to lead within a very short space of time – just over a month – to the Armageddon of World War One. It was, in fact, on 28 June 1914 that Franz Ferdinand was assassinated, the very date of Eric's previous letter home.

In the event nothing very much happened for the better part of three or four weeks and it was not until the ultimatum to Serbia

* Reproduced in full in the Appendix.

30

from Austria-Hungary that this assassination became the 'spark that set Europe ablaze'. In any case Eric very soon passes on to other news. *Phyllis Tipping never came to tea on Monday which was a pity as we had a lot of German ladies on board for tea.*

7

On arrival at Immingham there were 400 tons of coal to be taken on board, which *took us twelve hours owing to our having to twist it in with the winches on board*. What a ghastly business it was coaling ship! The next event was going to Nottingham to a luncheon party where silver was to be presented. This included a silver model of the first *Nottingham*. Then 25 members of the Nottingham Navy League were to be entertained to lunch. Also 300 people were coming to tea and to see over the ship. They came by special train, presumably from Nottingham to Immingham, arriving at 1 p.m. and not leaving until 6 p.m. Eric did not relish having to entertain them for five hours!

When Eric next writes it is to his youngest sister, May, enclosing a newspaper cutting from the *Nottingham Guardian* concerning the presentation of the silver plate. The train taking the naval party from Grimsby to Nottingham took five and a half hours. On arrival at 12.30 p.m. the officers had lunch with the Mayor. Eventually, after a march past by the ratings, the presentation itself, and tea, they left Nottingham at 5.45 p.m., arriving back on board at 9.30 p.m. – a rather quicker journey than it was going the other way! The dreaded entertainment of the 300 on board took place a few days later. It rained towards the end and water leaked through the awnings. Although the Mayor and Corporation were given a grand luncheon on the quarter deck, the people of Nottingham were shown round the docks, which *must have been a miserable business in the pouring rain*. They were allowed on board at 3 p.m. and given tea on the quarter deck, and then the ship was *swarming with people everywhere, in the Captain's cabin, wardroom and cabins. We were very glad to see the last of them at 6.00 p.m. However, we decided they had enjoyed their visit despite the pouring rain, but their knowledge of the navy was appalling owing to their being so far from the sea.*

The ship left Immingham the following evening and arrived at Portland 36 hours later. Their next assignment was to Spithead for the Naval Review. By 29 July, when Eric writes to both his parents, Austria had just declared war on Serbia, and it was clear to Eric that the die had been cast: *It looks as though our trip to the Cape is off owing to the state of things on the Continent.* The ship was now at Devonport, filling with coal to capacity, and all officers and men on leave were being recalled. There were messengers all over the town recalling men who were on shore locally. Quite definitely there was a sense of crisis. *Things seem to be looking as black as ever they have looked and personally I think we are in for it at last this time, as I don't think that Russia is going to stand out of it and if she goes to war against Austria then the fat will be in the fire with a vengeance.* Then later, at the end of the same letter he says, *I rather think it is war this time.*

As it happened, two days later, on 31 July, both Russia and Germany ordered general mobilisation and by noon the following day they were at war. The day after, 2 August, German troops entered France. This is also the date of Eric's next letter, again to both parents – *since I last wrote things seem to have been happening a bit.* They had coaled ship with only half the men on board and so it was a long business lasting continuously from 2.30 p.m. until 6 a.m. *Most of the men were dropping off to sleep almost as they shovelled the coal.*

By noon on 31 July they had got all the officers and most of the men back from leave, although they were still about 30 or 40 adrift. They left an hour later for Sheerness, although their destination was altered whilst they were in the Downs and they went to a rendezvous somewhere in the Thames Estuary. There they met up with the *Shannon, Roxburgh, Natal, Liverpool* and *Falmouth.* Then they proceeded up north, *no-one knew where.* They then proceeded to clean the ship for action, lashing the rigging, getting all superfluous gear out of boats, and *the Lyddite shell was got up and fused ready for use.*

On Saturday night, 1 August, as soon as it was dark, they went to night defence stations. Everyone slept at their stations, but

There was not much sleep for anyone that night for, if we were not keeping watch, we were at our stations. I was lucky and got two hours. The following day was employed in preparing the ship *still more for war.* All sofas and chairs were got up on deck ready for landing, cabin doors were taken down, chests of drawers got up on deck. *In fact the Quarter Deck is piled with furniture ready to land . . . we shall probably throw a good deal overboard before we go into action.*

Their destination was Rosyth, and it sounds as though they were ready for business. It is a well-known fact that Winston Churchill, now First Lord of the Admiralty, had the fleet ready at battle stations well before hostilities commenced, and certainly this letter of Eric's bears this out because it is now 2 August, and still two days before Britain was actually at war: *We have not seen a paper lately but I hear that Russia has declared war on Austria, and Germany is making raids into France. If this is so it seems that the whole of Europe has gone mad and that we are the only nation that has no desire to go to war at all.*

If this remark seems a little smug, it is only fair to point out that, at this stage, Belgian neutrality had not been violated by Germany. It was the violation of this neutrality on 4 August that was the occasion for Britain entering the war. Nevertheless, one cannot help being amused now when Eric describes all this as being *very tiresome.* Once again we have this rather favourite Woodruff word. I do recall hearing that this very word was used by my grandfather, I regret to say, when one of his house servants had a sudden heart attack and died on the spot.

Anyhow, to Eric, the prospect of the outbreak of war was 'tiresome' because it came at a time when he was about to go on leave. However, he follows this up with: *I have no wish to fight Germany at all, but if we do we shall be ready for them, and this may make them hesitate.* His final remark in this letter is interesting, if also amusing: *I should like you to keep this letter* confidential *as much as possible, and not let any foreigners read it as you never know, and can trust no-one.* Somehow I cannot imagine my grandparents distributing family correspondence to foreigners!

8

In the event, war was declared on 4 August, the day after the bank holiday, and in order to see how this affected Eric, I have to refer to a letter dated 27 September 1914, which was written by Eric from the then family home, Quarr Hill, Binstead, Isle of Wight, to his brother Shedden, who was then in Australia. (Shedden was to join the Australian Army in due course and he fought on the Western Front in the ranks. I can remember his telling me his experiences of being at Passchendaele in 1917.) The start of Eric's letter is interesting: *I am now home on six weeks' leave in order to recuperate after my operation for appendicitis, so for the present I am quite out of everything, and only saw about a week of the war.* However, he then tells Shedden how he had been very much looking forward to going out to the Cape Station in South Africa, where he would probably have remained about two or three years. Of course, the war *knocked all that on the head.*

He goes on to tell Shedden that on Monday, 3 August, they stopped in harbour all day and rested after working all day and night for two days, with some of the men only having had two hours' sleep over this period. On Tuesday they went to sea with orders to search for German armed merchant cruisers, reported to be in the North Sea. They had received a signal from the Admiralty saying that Britain's ultimatum to Germany expired at midnight. *That night I was on the bridge and then at 11.45 p.m. a signal came from the King and at midnight we got the signal from the Admiralty to commence hostilities against Germany.*

It was then apparently discovered that a lot of trawlers were laying mines in the North Sea. The only incident that occurred as far as Eric was concerned was with a Dutch trawler which took some stopping. No notice was taken of a signal, blank charges, or rifle shots, and it was only after a second shot across her bows from one of HMS *Nottingham*'s six-inch guns that she stopped. Eric and another officer, with a party, went over in a boat, armed with rifles and revolvers, to examine her. They were quite friendly, although they could not or would not speak English. Having found nothing suspicious, they gave the Dutch ship the necessary papers and departed. Eric felt that they were totally unaware on the Dutch trawler that war had been declared as they had apparently been at sea for several days.

After that they returned to harbour to coal ship and in consequence could not go out with the other cruisers to look for a supposed German base off the Norwegian coast. There was no question about it, the Royal Navy was indeed prepared. It was during the coaling that Eric felt a violent pain in his inside. It stayed with him all night. The next morning the doctor saw him and he was kept in bed, Fortunately for him, the ship remained in harbour owing to a temporary breakdown of the engines. In the evening the pain had *settled down in my right side* and the doctor suspected an appendicitis. That evening Eric was sent to a hospital ship in the harbour and he was operated on that night. He remained in the hospital ship for a week and was then sent to Queensferry Hospital, where he remained for a month. After five weeks from the time of his operation, he was sent home by train. His father met him at King's Cross and took him home. He was on six weeks' sick leave and was due at the Haslar Hospital on 22 October to be 're-surveyed', after which he hoped to return to the *Nottingham. I cannot walk about much yet but manage to walk about the garden and short distances slowly,* he says. *I go about in the motor a good deal. It is a very nice looking car and most comfortable, and later on I hope to be able to drive it.* Appendicitis was a much longer business then. My own son came out of hospital after half a week and it only took about a fortnight for him to be fully on his feet again.

Eric gives quite a vivid picture of comings and goings in the Solent, with a certain amount of exaggeration! *The whole of England is getting inundated with German prisoners, and yesterday some were landed at Ryde. Thousands of wounded are being landed at Southampton daily, and the port is now closed to commercial traffic, and the Solent is thick with transports of all shapes and sizes.* He then states how great the enthusiasm is in Britain for the war, with recruits flocking to the colours daily. Then he comes out with a rather typical, albeit somewhat arrogant comment: *If only the German Fleet would come and fight, we could wipe them out in a few minutes. As it is we shall have to find some means of digging them out.* Otherwise everything is normal; no rise in the price of food, with merchant ships coming and going as they please. Finally he tells Shedden that he has been promoted to full Lieutenant (his last promotion, as it happened, until 1922), and that he is now earning ten shillings a day.

The latest date referred to in this letter to his brother is 22 October, when he says he is due at the Haslar Hospital to be 're-surveyed', a strange word for a patient, even a naval officer. However, quite obviously the 're-survey' must have been satisfactory, because we find in a diary of his, dated 25 October 1914, that he is at Scapa Flow in the Orkneys. He had come over that morning on the mail steamer from Thurso, which left at 4 a.m. This does seem to be an unreasonable time, but it probably was dependent on the time of the arrival of the train at Thurso from Inverness. My own study of the Highland Railway at this time reveals that their somewhat limited services do seem to have been run at rather ungodly times. Anyhow, Eric crossed over with two RNR AP's and an 'old gent'. Were they the only passengers? He seems to have left them behind on arrival because he alone got the drifter *Lillian Maude*, which took him out to the *Nottingham*.

The ship was just in and was coaling. *Everyone seemed pleased to see me and I had the day off to settle in. Found my cabin in an awful mess owing to four 'snotties'* [midshipmen] *having lived in it.* Anyhow, he was quite ready by the evening when he took the first watch, but he turned in at midnight. The following day produced a drama on board. It was discovered that four percussions caps were missing, a very serious matter. The Captain addressed the men and left it to them to find the 'traitor', and stated in no uncertain terms that if he was brought before him he would be shot. In the future, sentries with loaded rifles would be placed at the guns with orders, if necessary, to shoot on sight. *It is not a very pleasant thought to think that we may have a traitor in our midst.*

The ship remained in harbour that day and the following one, although they went over to the other side of the Flow to their winter quarters near the depot ships at Long Hope. A court of inquiry was held on board regarding the percussion caps and Eric was called in to give evidence as he had kept watch from 11.00 to 12.00 on Sunday night. The following day, 28 October, the ship received a signal to raise steam for 18 knots with all dispatch, and they went to sea at 5 p.m. They proceeded to a spot 120 miles from Fair Isle on a direct line between Fair Isle and Heligoland, which was, of course, German territory. However, they saw nothing. The weather had now changed for the worse. A nasty sea got up and in consequence Eric felt pretty ill, not having been at sea for so long. By Friday the weather had improved. Still nothing of importance occurred and they were now north of Shetland. The weather changed for the worse again and it was very uncomfortable with the ship rolling and pitching. They were warned to look out for hostile aircraft and submarines reported in the neighbourhood. They were also passing through a possible minefield – all of which Eric describes as *altogether quite cheering news.*

However, all was well because the following morning at 8 a.m. they were back in Scapa Flow for coaling. His hold took in 350 tons. That evening they received a signal saying *Commence hostilities against Turkey.* Turkey had now joined the Central Powers. Eric had his own comment to make: *Very foolish of Turkey, who have been quite taken in by Germany.* For all this, one wonders how much opportunity *Nottingham* had of 'commencing hostilities against Turkey' up in the northern waters of Scapa Flow!

The following day, Sunday, 1 November, was given over to cleaning the ship after the coaling on Saturday, prayers and paying the men. On the Monday the Commodore, Goodenough, came aboard the ship and spoke about the seriousness of the loss of the percussion caps.

HMS *Southampton* left for Cromarty and so HMS *Nottingham* was now in charge of the LCS (Light Cruiser Squadron). One rather nice touch at this stage was that Captain Miller assembled all hands to say how satisfied he was with the appearance of the ship, which was very creditable considering the work they had been doing. Possibly he had received a pat on the back from the Commodore which he was just passing on. Nevertheless, it is the sort of thing which is done too seldom and which always acts as a boost to morale.

On Tuesday, 3 November, there is some excitement. There is a rumour that four German battleships are out in the North Sea, and they, along with other cruisers, are to join the First Battle Cruiser Squadron in attempting to intercept them. The weather was now bad again and Eric was obviously concerned because he was prone to seasickness. However, before sailing this time he took Mothersill, presumably as an antidote to seasickness, and it appeared to do the trick because he was not actually ill at all and was able to eat a good dinner despite the rolling, Having put to sea, they proceeded first to Cromarty to join up with the *Southampton – which, I suppose does not want to be left out if there is a scrap.* But before reaching Cromarty they received orders to return to Scapa Flow, where they arrived on the morning of 4 November. Then it was coaling again, although only 140 tons this time, and a mere two-hour job! What really put Eric out at this stage was that he received news that he was being transferred to the *Zealandia – which does not suit me at all especially as I hear that the Captain is an out and outer.* His own captain, Captain Miller, wrote to the Admiralty to try to get it cancelled, but he was afraid it was too late and would not do much good. However, he hoped for the best. The following day a signal came from the Commodore, discharging him in order to take up his new appointment. The reason he had not officially received news of his transfer is explained in his diary. On 6 November he received a letter from his mother and sister telling him that the news was sent to his home, where the Admiralty still thought he was. His mother and father had returned the letter to the Admiralty saying that Eric had already rejoined the *Nottingham.* Despite a last-minute attempt by Captain Miller to keep him, the signal came through and he had to go.

So ended one of the happiest six months in the service. I shall always believe I have left part of myself behind in the 'Nottingham'. My heart was heavy to see them going to sea tonight without me I wonder what they are going to do and whether I shall miss any of the fun. I went on board the 'Imperieuse' and slept the night there. There was no cabin so I slept in a cot. They seemed fairly decent fellows on board, mostly retired officers and RNR people, altogether funny old fogeys.

As it turned out he was to return to the *Nottingham* rather sooner than he had expected or hoped.

The following morning he left for Thurso at 11 a.m. on the steamer which took the fleet's mail to Thurso, and presumably this went direct from the Flow. It took two and a half hours. (Compare this with the two hours now taken by the P & O vessel from Stromness to Thurso.) On his way across, Eric saw three seaplanes flying around. The harbour for Thurso is, in fact, Scrabster, which he calls 'Crabster', but that may be just a misprint. He was driven in what he describes as a *funny antiquated old motor* to Thurso. One would have thought that no vehicle could have been in existence long enough then to be so described! He lunched at the Station Hotel (no longer in existence) and took the 2.45 p.m. train to Inverness. It did not leave until 3.30 p.m. and no reason is given for this. He describes the journey as being very long and tedious, although there was pretty scenery on the moors. I have to say that I myself have never found this train journey tedious, but rather fascinating. However, when one considers that until comparatively recently this journey took about six hours and the only refreshment, at Bonar Bridge, was tea and a bun, one can well understand the tedium! No longer can refreshment be obtained at Bonar Bridge (now renamed Ardgay), although there is generally a trolley of goodies on the train itself, what the French call a *vente ambulante*.

So Eric reached Inverness at 10.30 p.m. It needs to be said at this stage that the journey by rail from Thurso to Inverness is almost twice as long as the proverbial crow's route. He reported to the mail officer at the Queensgate Hotel, who was expecting him and gave him his 'appointment', whatever that meant. Quite obviously he could proceed no further that night, so he spent the night at the hotel. The following morning, Sunday, 8 November, he arose at 8.30 a.m., breakfasted and got his warrant to take him to Portland, where the *Zealandia* was. Once again the train was late leaving, being due out at 10.10 a.m. but not going until 10.35 a.m. This was still a Highland Railway line in those days, although it would become part of LMS within ten years. Its punctuality record was never very good, and later we shall find Eric speaking some fairly harsh words about it.

Once again he describes the journey as tedious, albeit with pretty scenery. He managed to get a luncheon basket at Kingussie and the train reached Perth at 3.40 p.m. This meant the journey had taken five hours. Nowadays the diesel multiple units do it in half the time. He managed to get a cup of tea at Perth before leaving the Highland Railway and joining the North British Railway for the journey from Perth to Edinburgh. It was a good connection, with the Edinburgh train leaving at 4.10 p.m. and arriving at 6 p.m. – not quite such a noticeable difference in timing here. It now takes one hour and a quarter.

Eric had dinner at the North British Hotel, and then arranged for a sleeper to King's Cross, which departed at 7.45 p.m. He arrived at 7.30 a.m. and proceeded to Waterloo, where he deposited his baggage in the cloakroom before telephoning the Bousfields at Denmark Hill to ask if he could come to breakfast. Permission granted, he took a taxi there. Being short of money, he managed to get a cheque for two pounds cashed by Dr Bousfield. That amount would not have gone far today! He went with Alec, Dr Bousfield's son, to the bank at Camberwell Green and then took a taxi to Gieves to purchase an oilskin, his previous one having been lost or stolen at Scapa Flow, a souwester and seaboots. Alec was Eric's brother-in-law. He had married Violet, Eric's eldest sister, and served in France in the Gunners. He was much the same age as Eric and died, well on in his eighties, in 1975. Eric returned to Waterloo for the 12.30 p.m. to Weymouth and managed to get lunch on the train. There was a pleasant companion in his compartment, an officer of the Sherwood Foresters who had been wounded in the leg and was now joining Kitchener's Army. This almost suggests he had to re-enlist.

41

9

Eric eventually arrived on board *Zealandia* at 6 p.m. and went to see the Captain, the 'out and outer', but he makes no mention of that in his diary. He soon settled down and they seemed a *decent set of fellows on board*. However, he realises he is now part of the Channel Fleet that *never goes to sea, a pretty cheery prospect for anyone wanting to see anything of the war*!

The following morning Eric was shown round his 'division' by Middleton, the sub lieutenant. He notes that watchkeeping is not going to be very strenuous after the *Nottingham* since there are six of them to do it. For the following two days, he writes, *nothing of importance occurred*, and he decides that he will now have to write this always, although on the third day, 13 November, they did at least go to sea. Their destination was Rosyth via the west coast of Ireland, definitely the long way round, but this was because of possible mines in the Dover Straits. Despite rough seas, he finds the motion as nothing compared with the *Nottingham*. His present ship, the *Zealandia*, was a battleship, which would have been the reason for this. Nevertheless, he is still saying 'thank you' to Mothersill: *I shall never go to sea without it*.

On Sunday, 15 November, Eric sadly and laconically reports, *We unfortunately killed a Chief Stoker today. He was in the coal shute locker when, owing to the motion of the ship they* [presumably the coals] *fell on him, and pinned him to the deck killing him*. There seem to have been far too many accidents of this nature in the days when ships were powered by coal. It really was rough now, and they were only making four knots; everything had to be battened down. The ship went into Berehaven, in the south-west of Ireland, until the weather moderated. The wind dropped the following morning and they proceeded. The only event mentioned is the burial at sea of the Chief Stoker. The next day they passed St Kilda's, which was still inhabited in those days. Then, believe it or not, it was back to Scapa Flow, where they anchored at about 8 a.m. on Wednesday, 18 November, exactly 11 days after Eric had left. However, they were off again within 24 hours, well escorted because of submarines. Now they were in the North Sea they were much more likely to be attacked. However, nothing exciting occurred and they arrived safely at Rosyth at 8 a.m. on Wednesday, 20 November.

Eric received a pleasant surprise with the mail to the effect that he got his appointment to the *Nottingham* once again. *Great was my joy at this unexpected good luck, and although they are very nice fellows on the 'Zealandia', I am pretty glad at the thought of returning to my friends of the 'Nottingham'*. His comments sound almost as if they have come straight out of the *Boy's Own Paper*, but possibly people really did express themselves like that 80 years ago.

Eric packed up and managed to leave the ship at 2 p.m. the following day, 21 November. He reached Edinburgh at 4 p.m. and as there was no train to Inverness that evening, it was back to the North British Hotel once again. Then he had tea at Fullers with Watson, a fellow officer who had also left the *Zealandia* and was joining a submarine at Leith, and after dinner at the hotel he finished the day at the cinema.

The following morning he caught the 7.30 a.m. to Perth, where he changed on to the Highland Line. He managed to obtain a luncheon basket at Kingussie, for which he was grateful, having only had a hurried tea and toast before leaving Edinburgh. *It was very cold on the journey, all the hills being covered with snow and the ponds frozen over*. Words like 'lochs' and 'mountains' do not seem to come easily to him. He reached Inverness at 2 p.m. and, having reported to the mail officer at the Queensgate Hotel, found out that the *Nottingham* was at Scapa Flow. So he carried on north on the 4 p.m. to Thurso, *a terribly tedious journey, the train getting later and later*. Of course, it would have been dark all the way. He was saved from starvation because he was able to obtain a tea basket, once again at Bonar Bridge. The train arrived at Thurso at 12.30 a.m., *about four and a half hours late*. I feel this may be something of an exaggeration, since I should doubt whether as little as four hours in those days would have been the train's official schedule, For all that, eight and a half hours in the dark and quite probably with inadequate heating would have been extremely tedious, to say the least.

Eric and two other naval officers managed to get into the Royal Hotel, which also provided supper for them (not bad at 12.30 a.m.) However, since the *Fleet Messenger* was due to leave Scrabster at 5 a.m., it was to be a short night for them. He was up at 4.15 a.m., and the hotel supplied tea and eggs, again not bad! (In all fairness I must point out that the Pentland Hotel, also in Thurso, provided me with breakfast at 5.15 a.m. in November 1991.)

The crossing appears very long for some reason, because they did not come alongside the *Imperieuse* until 9 a.m. However, *Nottingham* was at sea and would not be in for another two or three days. There being no accommodation on the *Imperieuse*, Eric was put up aboard the *Cambria*, originally an LNWR ferry on the Holyhead – Kingston run, but then in wartime, chartered to the Admiralty for running dispatches.

Not until Thursday, 26 November, did Eric manage to board the *Nottingham*. Before this came news of the ramming of a German submarine trying to get into Scapa Flow. When he returned to *Nottingham*, he inevitably found her coaling, since the ship was due for trawler patrol on the morrow. *Everybody pleased to see me back again*, he was glad to discover. The purpose of these trawler patrols was to hunt for German submarines and it was a trawler which had rammed the U-boat a few days before.

During the next ten days or so there was nothing unusual to report. The days were spent on the usual sort of duties patrolling and coaling. It was his birthday on 7 December; he was 22, and was pleased to receive a great 'budget' of letters from home. Other than that there was only coaling.

Four days later came news of the sinking of *Scharnhorst* and *Gneisenau*, along with *Leipzig* and *Nürnberg*. He almost talks as though this is the last of the German fleet. It is interesting that the first two of these ships which he names were to appear (in name) again in World War II.

The *Nottingham* switched stations from Scapa Flow to Rosyth, *some day soon after Dec.13th* and on Christmas Eve they all received the news that they were to go to sea, *So there won't be any Christmas for us this year.* By Christmas they were at action stations. *The whole navy has put to sea in order that we shall not be caught napping at Christmas festivities.* The Admiralty had received information that a strong German force was coming out in order to raid the east coast. Everybody was now in high spirits, out in the North Sea with the battle cruisers. Four destroyers reported having sighted the German ship *Roon* and some German destroyers steering east, so they all proceeded east, only to get a further signal saying that the German battle cruisers were bombarding Scarborough. They therefore turned right round and proceeded at full speed, going right through a German minefield in order to get there quicker. Unfortunately, they were too far south and the German ships escaped north and got away without being sighted. *It is believed that the whole High Seas Fleet had come out in support of their cruisers and, if we had only met them there would probably have been a general action and by now most of the German fleet would have been sunk.* As it was, there was *great sickness at having missed the Germans, who must have been well informed of our whereabouts to have escaped so easily.*

The next day, Christmas Day, was spent at sea, sweeping between Scarborough and Heligoland. *Birmingham* and *Southampton* reported seeing submarine periscopes, but whether 'ours' or 'theirs' they could not tell. On Boxing Day they received orders to return to base, and they anchored off Rosyth at 2.15 a.m. on 27 December. Then, when it was light – no prizes for a correct guess! – they coaled ship. On 28 December they celebrated Christmas and, despite fears of having to go to sea in the middle of it, they held a concert in the dog watches (5.30–7.30 p.m.) and then had their Christmas dinner, with the Captain as chief guest. The rest of the evening was spent singing songs, *which was mostly done by the Commander.*

Eric comments on how much more secure they felt in harbours like Rosyth and Cromarty, where they were protected by outside forts and a boom, *so much better than Scapa Flow*. This was ominously prophetic in a way, although it was not until the winter of 1939, in the early stages of World War II, that this point could have been said to have been made, when a German submarine got into the Flow and sank the battleship *Royal Oak*. The answer was, of course, the Churchill Barriers, completed with the aid of Italian POWs in 1943. However, in the light of these later events, Eric's feelings of security make interesting reading.

There was little or nothing to report during the next week, and they remained in harbour. Nevertheless, it was necessary to coal ship on the last day of the year!

Eric saw the new year in while on first watch. Then 2 January 1915 brought news of the sinking of HMS *Formidable* in the Channel. On 3 January they were at sea again. Before they set off, they had received signals to say that Zeppelins had been sighted over Crowborough and Chelmsford. The combination of the two places seems strange. One has to suppose these just happened to be the first two places to send in reports. All the same, there was not very much which the Light Cruiser Squadron at Rosyth, in the Forth, could do about it! Having come out to sea, they got their orders during the first watch, *that we had come out for nothing and were to do some firing practice before returning to harbour.*

Then there was an alarm that there were some enemy destroyers in the vicinity and everything was cleared away in readiness. But *they only proved to be some patrol vessels.* One presumes they were friendly! Frustration again, nor did it help next day with a fierce wind blowing east-south-east: *Did not feel well all day.* They had to stay out without doing their firing practice, which was postponed until the following day, *very annoying as I think we go to sea quite enough already.* They got their firing done the following day, and for the next few days there was little apart from coaling, and a route march for the men – presumably to keep them occupied.

On 9 January a store-ship came alongside with presents from the City of Nottingham. Every officer and man received a Christmas card from the City and County of Nottingham, and a present as well, consisting of 2 lbs of plum pudding, 1 lb of Cadbury's block chocolate in a sealed tin, one pair of mittens, one pair of bootlaces, one tin of dubbin, ten plain postcards with lead pencil, one packet of Formaloids for the throat, one tin of peppermints, fifty cigarettes, one tablet of soap, one packet of caramels, one tin of boracic ointment, and one tin of Vaseline. It certainly was, as Eric says, very generous. They were all now set up for small pleasures and minor ailments, quite apart from being able to service their boots in wet weather!

Two days later the crew received another Christmas gift. This was Princess Mary's present, consisting of an artistic tin box containing tobacco, cigarettes, a pipe, a Christmas card and a photo of Princess Mary, *altogether a nice little souvenir*. This would have been Princess Mary, the previous Princess Royal, the only daughter of George V and Queen Mary, who became Countess of Harwood. Whilst on National Service I once met a soldier from a Scottish regiment whose unit had more than once been inspected by her in the early 1950s. She was quite a martinet, or so it seemed to me when the soldier told how, when she inspected the rear ranks, she would stop and make a deliberate point of inspecting the backs of the brass buckles on the webbing belts. It is interesting to see that her present was entirely directed towards the smoker. I never remember seeing Eric smoking during the time I knew him, but he may well have done so then, in 1915. Certainly the assumption seemed to be that most people did smoke. It would hardly go down so well today if a similar present was given.

So the routine continued. *Thursday, 12th January. In harbour. The third Battle Cruiser Squadron went to sea in the evening. What for, I do not know, but I do not think that it was for anything particular.* He was quite right, because when, nearly a week later, they went out on patrol, they passed the third Battle Cruiser Squadron returning to harbour, having carried out firing practice! They did their own patrol, returned to harbour, coaled ship and went out again, this time with the battle cruisers behind them, *so I suppose there is some stunt on.* This proved to be the case. Apparently they had learnt from Intelligence that a German patrol was in the habit of patrolling between Heligoland and the mouth of the River Ems. The aim was for three light cruisers and a large number of destroyers to cut these vessels off in the Heligoland

Bight and bring them into action.

On the morning of 19 January they arrived in Heligoland Bight. Everyone was in high spirits, owing to the likelihood of at last meeting with something. However, it was not to be. After steaming about all the forenoon they saw nothing except a Zeppelin a long way off, *who, on seeing us turned and made off in the opposite direction.* About 11 a.m., *Admiral Beatty made a signal to the Commodore which said 'We have no luck and suppose we must return home'. This we did and course was shaped northward amidst great disappointment.* However else one may feel about war, one cannot get away from the fact that the morale of the men on the spot is enhanced incredibly by the prospect of action. The reverse is equally true – that the prospect of inaction is a blow to morale. So it was back to harbour, with its routine of firing practice and the inevitable coaling.

10

On 23 January Eric took the opportunity of going to Edinburgh. It is interesting that they were informed that they went 'at their own risk', if they missed the ship because it had had to go to sea suddenly. One wonders what the risk meant. Was it that they would be posted absent in this event and therefore liable to disciplinary action? This seems hard to believe. Probably it is more likely that the risk was that they might miss the chance of action.

Five of them set off together. They started out in the tug and caught the 1.07 p.m. train, probably from South Queensferry, and they were in Edinburgh by 1.30 p.m. They went straight to the North British Hotel to see if there was any telegram recalling them. There was not, but even so they could only have had about two hours in town. They spent their time shopping, and looked into the US Club before returning on the 4.07 p.m. train. While on the train, they heard that all officers from Battle Cruiser and Light Cruiser Squadrons were recalled, so they were concerned as to whether they would be back in time. On the train, Eric met a Mr Reed, who had been a master at Osborne and Dartmouth and was now in the RNVR as a lieutenant on the *Tiger*. As a final comment to this expedition to Edinburgh, he says rather strangely, *I forgot to mention that whilst in Edinburgh we had great difficulty in getting rid of Wiltshire, and eventually did this by being excessively rude to him.* One's imagination boggles at this – Wiltshire was one of the party of five officers who had set out together.

They were back on board soon after 5 p.m. and found everything ready for going to sea, which they did at 6 p.m. They proceeded at 20 knots, going south with the battle cruisers astern. *There is evidently some big stunt on as they have got out the whole Grand Fleet.* In their haste to get south they actually went through part of a minefield in order to cut a corner. The information was that a force of German cruisers was about to make a raid on the east coast. *We must evidently have an extremely good spy in Germany, as we get most accurate information, which generally proves correct.*

What followed was the naval action known since as the Dogger Bank Incident. It is interesting to note that, according to *Encyclopaedia Britannica* for 1930, Vice Admiral Beatty left the Forth at 6 p.m. on 23rd January, and that the German Admiral Hipper had simply been sent out to 'reconnoitre off the Dogger Bank', because 'reports from America at the time had led the Germans to think that a plan for blocking their harbours was afoot'. It also goes on to state that before the German ships set off 'their strength and intentions had been revealed by their own wireless'. This rather refutes Eric's view that it was due to British intelligence. Eric himself describes the coming battle in an *Account of the Action with the German Battle Cruisers.* The German force consisted of four battle cruisers and four light cruisers, respectively referred to as 1st and 2nd Scouting Group. The British response was five battle cruisers (First and Second Battle Cruiser Squadron) and four light cruisers, of which *Nottingham* was one (First Light Cruiser Squadron). However, this comparative balance of forces was heavily swayed by three light cruisers and thirty destroyers of the Harwich Flotilla, which formed up with Beatty's force when the action commenced. In heavy guns Beatty was decidedly superior. In speed too his squadron had the initiative.

Eric had just turned in – *to get an hour's sleep* – when he heard a commotion outside. On asking the sentry, he was told that action stations had been sounded. He hurried up on deck to the after control, where he assisted the First Lieutenant. Everything was cleared away ready. Apparently firing had been heard on the horizon. *This I afterwards learnt was the 'Undaunted' and some Destroyers which had met the force of German Battle Cruisers and had been fired on, both the 'Undaunted' and the 'Meteor' being damaged.* The *Encyclopaedia Britannica* records *Meteor* sustaining one hit with four killed and one wounded, although there is no mention about *Undaunted*. It is just possible that it has been mistaken for the *Aurora*, which is listed as receiving two hits. All three ships, *Meteor, Undaunted* and *Aurora*, belonged to the Harwich Flotilla.

However, there now seems to have been a lull, and since everything had been cleared away and got ready on *Nottingham*, they were all piped to breakfast – *Much to our joy because no one likes fighting on an empty stomach. We all went and made a hearty breakfast, everyone in the highest spirits on account of the proximity of the enemy.* Once again morale was boosted by the prospect of action. There seems no question about it. One cannot help wondering whether it is the first prospect of action which is the cause of the morale boost. I question whether the men in the trenches were so enthusiastic for their next bout of action 'over the top'.

During this time they were steaming full speed towards the enemy and at about 8.45 a.m. they went to action stations with the enemy well in sight. Full steam would, it seems, have been about 25.5 knots. By this time, according to *Encyclopaedia Britannica*, the action involving other ships had been going on for one and a half hours. *Kolburg*, a German light cruiser, had retired from action at 7.45 a.m. At the sound of the guns, Beatty had ordered the light cruisers to chase to the south. The *Southampton* sighted the German battle cruisers at 7.50 a.m. and Hipper, having been taken by surprise, turned south-east and ran for home. All told, he was heavily outnumbered, although whether he was actually aware of it then is more doubtful. Home was Heligoland, 140 miles away.

Beatty was in the battle cruiser *Lion*, with the rest of the First Squadron, in pursuit. The Light Cruiser Squadron appears to have been on a parallel course. Owing to a superiority of speed, Beatty was closing the gap. At around this stage Eric says he saw, on the horizon, four large battle cruisers and three light cruisers ahead of them, *steaming roughly South East as hard as they could go.* There is nothing to say so, but the implication is that these were German ships.

Meanwhile, our Battle Cruisers, consisting of the Flagship

'Lion', with 'Tiger', 'Princess Royal', 'New Zealand' and 'Indomitable' had gone to the South and separated from us, but they were now coming up astern of the German ships as hard as they could steam. We Light Cruisers, 'Southampton', 'Birmingham' and 'Nottingham' and 'Lowestoft' steamed a parallel course to the enemy, keeping them on the starboard bow. The 'Lion' was the first to open fire.

According to *Encyclopaedia Britannica* this took place at 8.42 a.m., seven minutes after *Nottingham* had gone to action stations, according to Eric's account, and seems perfectly feasible.

The first shots fell short and very soon the German ships started to reply. *As far as I could see their shots were very accurate.* One suspects that this could well have been true, perhaps the first indication of what was going to cause Beatty to say in his frustration at Jutland over a year later, 'What's wrong with our bloody guns!' Possibly it simply was that the German naval artillery was better. On this occasion the Germans scored their first hit on *Lion* at 9.28 a.m., sending an 11-inch shell through her waterline aft. However, a quarter of an hour later *Seydlitz*, the flagship, received a more devastating hit from a 13.5-inch shell which penetrated the after turret and, exploding inside, set fire to the charges in the working chamber. In the meantime, *Bluecher* was having trouble with her engines and at 10 a.m. drew out of the line, labouring heavily.

Eric seems to have been a spectator from a distance. When the enemy ships opened fire Eric thought they were firing at them, but, *Since we saw no shots falling anywhere, we realised that they were firing back at our Battle Cruisers. From our unique position, nearly on the beam, we had a most magnificent view of the fight and were able to signal to our Battle Cruisers the fall of their shot. This was particularly useful in the case of 'Tiger' as she was firing perfectly lovely salvos but they were all going over, and we were able to tell her this. As far as I could see we were the first to get a hit as a fire was seen to break out on one of the enemy. At this we cheered and clapped but they soon put it out.*

He gives credit where he thinks it is due with, *some of the German ships were firing beautiful ripple salvos and must have obtained hits on our ships as their fire seemed both rapid and accurate.* At one time he says they got in too close and *I think it was the 'Bluecher' which opened fire on us . . . some of their shots pitched in the sea about three hundred yards away giving out a blackish smoke which made me think they were using common shell.*

Some of the *Bluecher*'s shots passed right over them and nearly hit the *Lowestoft*. *Nottingham* altered course in order to get out of range, and just as well because a shell pitched in the sea astern of *Birmingham* where the *Nottingham* would have been if it had not done so. Understandably they had been waiting to get at the enemy light cruisers, but *this was impossible owing to their position ahead of the Battle Cruisers, and they evidently got orders to make for home as quickly as possible because they were going much too fast to catch them.*

Nevertheless, the battle cruiser fight continued fast and furious. The smoke from exploding shells, the guns and the funnels was now so great that you could barely distinguish the ships, but it was seen that one of them had evidently been crippled for she was dropping rapidly astern. This would appear to have been the *Bluecher*. Looking at our other record we read that at 10.30 a.m. a salvo fell on *Bluecher*, a shell penetrated the central ammunition passage, setting fire to the cartridges and sending a flash of flame through the fore turrets. The main steam pipe was damaged and her speed came down to 17 knots, and she gradually dropped behind, enveloped in smoke. The remainder of the enemy were clearly bent on escaping, as Eric suggested. Regarding the *Bluecher*, he is more dramatic about her difficulties: *It was then that she was doomed for she seemed to be out of control and had only one of her guns firing occasionally.*

Although the enemy was 'bent on escaping' they had apparently decided to do what damage they could, and to this end concentrated their fire on the *Lion*, which between 10.35 and 11.50 a.m. was repeatedly hit with heavy shell, with the result that she started to drop astern while the other battle cruisers raced past her. At 11.00 a.m. the flagship, *Lion*, received such heavy injuries that she was thrown out of the fight. Beatty, however, still retained control. Just before this the periscope of an enemy

53

submarine had been seen on the starboard bow and at 10.45 a.m., Beatty had made a signal to alter course eight points (90 degrees) to port to a course north by east. This was the initial cause of the action being broken off, but the usual submarine warning was not made by the *Lion*, thereby mystifying the other ships. This is interesting. Perhaps the usual submarine warning had not been given because there was, in fact, no submarine. But let us now turn to Eric's account.

We sighted what we thought to be a submarine on our port beam about five hundred yards away and we opened fire at it with one of our guns. It looked to me exactly like a submarine periscope that was coming to the surface after having discharged its torpedo, but I found out later that it was only a spar used for indicating drift nets.

Obviously one can never tell whether it is the same submarine, supposed or otherwise, but it is an interesting conjecture, especially because this was the initial cause of the engagement being broken off. However, there was still a considerable element of doubt as to what Beatty really intended. Further signals made at 11.02 a.m. were an endeavour by Beatty to get the squadron to turn back again three points to north-east, followed by a signal 'Attack the enemy's rear'. At the time this could only mean an instruction to attack the *Bluecher*, the only enemy ship bearing north-east, now disabled and drifting astern of her companions. The *Nottingham* now moved in for the kill.

As the 'Bluecher' was much closer to us now we opened fire on her and although we fired ninety-eight rounds at her, some of which I am sure hit her, which is not bad as we were firing pretty well at extreme range of our guns, that is about 12,000 yards. We never went less than 11,000 yards (i.e. six and a quarter miles). She ('Bluecher') had very few of her guns firing but now and again she got a round off, but they all fell short and latterly she devoted all her attention to our Battle Cruisers which were coming up fast astern, and soon all her guns ceased firing as, I presume, they were out of action.

By now, because of the misreading or otherwise of Beatty's signals, fire was concentrated on the *Bluecher*. Hipper, with the remainder of the German force, drew rapidly out of range. At 11.38 a.m. *Arethusa* came up and fired two torpedoes into the *Bluecher*. The whole thing seems a little reminiscent of the sinking of the *Bismarck* in May 1941.

Eric noted from the *Nottingham* that the battle cruiser *Tiger* came up at full speed, with smoke pouring out of her three large funnels and belching forth fire from her foremost guns, at the doomed German ship. *The extraordinary thing was that where we were the ship did not look so badly damaged, but close to she must have looked an awful sight.* There is a terrible sense of vultures round their prey! If so, Eric appears to blame the other German ships: *The enemy's Battle Cruisers had evidently left the* Bluecher *to her fate because they now put on full speed and disappeared over the horizon, and we could never hope to catch them.* However, he does suggest that the enemy battle cruisers had been keeping back a bit in order to screen the *Bluecher* as much as possible, but when they saw they could not save her they dashed for home.

He then pays tribute to the enemy by saying, *There was no doubt that their two Battle Cruisers are a bit faster than ours but not so heavily armed.* However, although the armament is confirmed, according to the record the average top speed of British battle cruisers was 27.2 knots, while that of the Germans was 25.5 knots.

By this time, *Bluecher* had ceased firing and was *listing heavily, ablaze fore and aft, and she sank at 12.13 p.m.* Hipper was now out of sight some 15 miles off, and so the British battle cruisers formed into lines ahead and steered westwards, i.e. home. This is borne out by Eric: *Our Battle Cruisers did not attempt to follow, although we kept on our course for a time.* He has one final comment about the *Bluecher* and her crew:

When we last saw her she was a pitiful sight and one could not help feeling sorry for the poor wretches on board as she refused to surrender, and so we had to sink her by pouring broadside after broadside at close range into her hull. She was

*evidently badly on fire amidships as clouds of smoke and steam
were rising up from her. When we turned and made for the spot
where she was, she was surrounded by Destroyers and a Light
Cruiser of the 'Arethusa' class was picking up survivors.
Altogether one hundred and twenty three survivors were picked
up including the Captain.*

What about the British ships? HMS *Lion* had been severely
damaged. During the early stages the Germans had concentrated
their fire on her and she had fallen behind. Beatty had transferred
his flag to the destroyer *Attack* and later, at 12.30 p.m. to the
Princess Royal, of his own Battle Cruiser Squadron. By this time
warning had been received of the approach of the German High
Seas Fleet, so he gave up all hope of renewing the action. Eric
was left wondering what had happened to *Lion*.

*It was now seen we had only four Battle Cruisers. We hoped
that she ['Lion'] was all right and we would come across her
when we retraced our course. How eagerly we looked for her,
for it would not be much success if we had lost her, but rather
the other way round. We sighted some Cruisers of the Third
Cruiser Squadron but no 'Lion', then, later on, much to our
joy, she appeared over the horizon looking much as usual, but
the 'Arethusa' reported she had a list.*

She seems to have been, in fact, in quite a bad way, only being
able to steam at eight knots, and later on not at all, on account of
leaky condensers, and so she was taken in tow by the
Indomitable. As she could only be towed at seven knots, there
was a fear that the enemy might send out destroyers to attack her,
so she was given a good screen of friendly destroyers and light
cruisers, of which *Nottingham* was one.

Eric is somewhat disparaging about *Indomitable*: *Being so
slow she never got into action at all except at the end when she
fired at the 'Bluecher'*. In actual fact her speed was exactly the
same as the *New Zealand* and fractionally faster than the
Bluecher.

In addition to the sinking of the *Bluecher*, hits were sustained
by *Seydlitz* (3), *Derflinger* (1) and *Kolberg* (2). On the British

Eric – aged 10 months.

Eric – aged about 7 years.

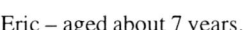

Above: Prep. School days.

Left: Osborne Naval Cadet.

Above: HMS *Cornwall.*

Left: Sub Lieutenant. 1912.

HMS *Nottingham.* 1912

First Lieutenant.

Eric with his family – wartime – about 1917.

Shedden, the elder brother who
served in the Australian forces.

HMS *Glorious.*

HMS *Cardiff* leading in the German Battle Cruisers, *Seydlitz, Moltke,* and *Hindenburg.*

German Battle Cruiser, *Hindenburg* in Firth of Forth, 21st November 1918.

German Battle Cruiser, *Hindenburg* – Scapa Flow, Orkneys, June 1928 – 'Scuttled'.

Eric with extended family – post-war – about 1920.

HMS *Hermes.*

Left: 'Picnicking'. 'On the China Station'.

Below: HMS *Furious* with attendant destroyers.

Above: HMS *Furious* with aeroplanes ranged up on deck.

Left: Lieutenant Commander Woodruff. 1930.

HE The Governor of Hong Kong flying round the New Territories in a Fairy IIID
Seaplane with Lt Cmdr. Woodruff on board as Observer.

Self   Brookman   Lentaigne

Canton. Christmas Eve 1926.

Picnic at Tolo Harbour near Hong Kong 1927. Eric is left of centre in jacket and topee.

Railway, North Borneo.

Labuan, North Borneo. Eric is in the stern of the boat.

Scenes from Ceylon (Sri Lanka).

Left: The 'Commander' – 2nd World War.

On MVF *Massabiele,* November 1941 – for trials of arming 'R' mine torts with dummy mines.

Above: Kirkwall, Orkney. Sea cadets marching past Lord Lieutenant. Eric is on the extreme left of the party of dignitaries. May 1945.

Left: In Dorset – At the Black Horse Inn, Teffont. August 1973.

side, apart from *Lion* being put out of action, *Tiger* received 7 hits, *Meteor* 1 and *Aurora* 2. German casualties were much higher, with 792 of the *Bluecher* crew killed and 45 wounded. On the British side, including *Lion*, there were only 14 killed and 21 wounded. In addition, 187 of the *Bluecher* crew were saved and taken prisoner. However, the reader does need to be reminded that the German ships were considerably outnumbered.

Finally, *Lion*, towed by the 'slow' *Indomitable*, reached Rosyth safely the next morning. *Nottingham* also made progress that seemed very slow. The following day, 25 January, they took station astern of the battle cruisers and proceeded towards the Firth of Forth. During the day they received a congratulatory signal from the King for the previous day's victory, and they reached their old billet at Rosyth at 5.30 a.m. the next morning, 26 January. They were glad to hear that the *Lion* had got safely into harbour, *So we can now call the fight on Sunday a victory as we have lost no ship of any kind. Our casualties were very small considering, only one officer was killed, and that was Captain Taylor in the* Tiger. *He used to be the Engineer Commander at Osborne and Dartmouth so I knew him.*

It certainly does seem that casualties were light as compared with those in the trenches. The *Daily Mirror* of 29 January 1915, whose headlines, front page and centre spread were taken up with the Dogger Bank Incident, elsewhere talks of enemy action on the Western Front with German losses of 20,000 in attacks celebrating the Kaiser's birthday on 27 January. The Allies conceded losses of 800. These figures may well be suspect in a newspaper, but even if one reverses the figures the point is made. One's chances of staying alive in the First World War were infinitely greater in the navy than they were in the army!

In his diary entry for the following day, Eric reports that there is discussion of the damage done to the German ships in the Dogger Bank Incident, apart from the *Bluecher*. This comes from eyewitness accounts from the *Lion*, and also from survivors from the *Bluecher*. There is also a suggestion that a German light cruiser, the *Kolburg* may have been sunk, but this, he is careful to state, has not been confirmed.

11

Eric's diary, which he had started on 25 October 1914 when he rejoined *Nottingham* after his convalescent leave, continues until 13 March. This period of just over six weeks was taken up in the main with patrol activity, the occasional false alarm, but no action as such. Quite frequently a day's entry in the diary is *In harbour. Nothing of importance occurred.*

After 13 March there is no further information from Eric, either correspondence with his family or in his own diary, until 12 December 1918. During this period the *Nottingham* was sunk, on 19 August 1916. Before this, however, there is reason to believe that the ship played its part at the Battle of Jutland on 31 May that same year. Amongst Eric's possessions is a postcard-size photograph of HMS *Birmingham*, on the back of which has been written *Battle of Jutland May 31st 1916. – splash of German salvo falling short of HMS Birmingham and over HMS Nottingham. Taken from HMS Nottingham.* This would certainly indicate that *Nottingham* was present at Jutland.

Regarding the sinking of the ship for some time I thought Eric had been on leave at the time. However, having recently unearthed a diary for 1916 written by Eric's father, I discovered an interesting entry for 19 August 1916: *Telegram from Eric from Jarrow saying all well so there must have been a battle in the North Sea.* Then on 21 August my grandfather (Eric's father) refers to it again: *Telegram from Eric from Devonport saying he would be home in a day or two. His ship, the Nottingham has been sunk by a torpedo in the North Sea.* The next entry in the diary is 29 August: *Eric arrived about lunchtime – very glad to see him again after his terrible experiences.* Two days later, according to the diary, Eric returned to Devonport. I think one

58

must assume from this that Eric was on the *Nottingham* when it went down. The only thing which is a little puzzling is that the very same day that the ship was sunk (19 August) Eric was able to send a telegram from Jarrow. However, if the sinking took place reasonably close to shore there is no reason why not, especially if there were other ships around to pick up survivors.

Eric is then listed as having joined HMS *Glorious* on 3 September 1916, with C.B. Miller as Captain. Whether all the surviving crew of the *Nottingham* were transferred to the *Glorious* I am unable to say. My own recollection of the *Glorious* is of an aircraft carrier which was sunk in the early years of World War II. I rather imagine it to have been an old battleship converted, similar to HMS *Courageous* and *Furious*, both of which were also sunk during the early part of World War II. When Eric wrote to his father on 12 November 1918, the notepaper is headed HMS *Glorious*, c/o GPO.

This letter starts somewhat dramatically, as is to be expected on that particular date:

I must take this opportunity of writing to you now that hostilities have ceased. I have just been reading the terms of the Armistice and must say they are very thorough and don't give Germany much of a loophole for escape. Some say they will not give up their fleet without a fight, but they have nothing to gain by it and we are ready for them at any time. How thankful we must all be that we have escaped with our lives. At the beginning of the war I never thought I should live to see the end, and Shedden I hope he is still alright, and now that the fighting has stopped he ought to be safe. That is another thing that we ought to be thankful for, that our family has come through all safe.

We in the navy celebrated the victory in proper naval fashion, he continues. *The men had a half holiday and we spliced the mainbrace.* All very clean and clinical, almost as though a naval regatta had just taken place. Eric finishes his letter, *We shall now have our work cut out to see that the terms of the Armistice are carried out.* This last remark almost makes the reader feel that Eric was personally responsible for the implementation of the

Armistice! He concludes by anticipating that Heligoland will have to be occupied, and that the Germans will not give up their ships without a certain amount of trouble. There is a final postscript to the letter, *Tremendous things are happening . . . War is over. Hurrah*!

The next letter, ten days later, is again from HMS *Glorious*, this time from Burntisland. Like Rosyth, Burntisland is on the northern side of the Firth of Forth, but about 15 miles to the east on the other side of the Forth Bridge. This time the letter is to his mother. He opens again fairly dramatically: *Tremendous things have happened since I last wrote. First of all the incredible has taken place, the German Navy has surrendered*! I think that Eric's view about this does represent a heartfelt feeling of relief, probably felt throughout the navy and, indeed, throughout the country as a whole.

Britain's predominance at sea had been firmly established during the eighteenth century, and during the nineteenth it had been unquestioned. However, the rise of Imperial Germany and her construction of a fleet to rival Britain's had been a shock to the system. The one main encounter between the two fleets at Jutland had been a drawn battle. More British ships were lost than German, although it was the German Fleet which retired to base and effectively stayed there for the remainder of the war, which did not do its morale any good. When the German Fleet surrendered, there may well have been a feeling in Britain of 'We are never going to give them the opportunity of threatening us again'. The main threat had been to Britain's prestige as the leading naval power, and Britain was determined to humiliate Germany in this respect in particular, without thought to the consequences. No one thought much further than having the surrendered German Fleet on show in Scapa Flow. There was a small-mindedness about the whole thing. Quite frankly one questions whether there were any plans about what to do with the German ships. In the end it was the Germans who made the plans, and scuttled the ships.

The plan for the surrender was that the German High Seas Fleet should meet its British counterpart at the entrance to the Firth of Forth.

Eric then describes the events of the surrender of the German Fleet as he saw it from Burntisland. Included among his possessions are some full-plate photographs of some of the German ships under steam on this occasion and, what is even more interesting, a plan of the whole sail past. This is a large chart showing the dispositions of all the ships involved. The chart is headed *Der Tag* (The Day). I think, but I may be wrong, that it was intended to inflict the maximum humiliation upon the enemy. Prior to the outbreak of war (and no doubt during its course) *Der Tag* was, to those German militarists who saw their newly built fleet as an aggressive challenge to Britain, the grand finale, the day when Britain's fleet was sunk in its entirety or else forced into a humiliating surrender. I believe that *Der Tag* had been the toast drunk in the wardroom of many a German warship.

The chart shows three vertical columns of ships coloured according to class of ship, the central column being the German High Seas Fleet, consisting of 21 ships (5 battle cruisers, 9 battleships and 7 cruisers). The two columns on either side consisted of 78 ships, with another 5 acting as escorts for the centre column. Of these ships there were 5 battleships from the USA – the *New York, Texas, Arkansas, Wyoming* and *Florida* – and one French cruiser, *Admiral Aube*. All the rest were Royal Navy. Perhaps some of the ships are worthy of comment, mainly because they played a part in the next war. Firstly there was the battleship *Royal Oak*, which would only survive a few months of the war in 1939 before being sunk, ironically enough, in Scapa Flow close to the graveyard of the German ships she was now escorting. Then the *Repulse* and the *Renown*, two battle cruisers which survived into the next war, although *Repulse* was to be sunk by Japanese aircraft off Malaya in December 1941. Finally *Warspite* did good work in the Second World War, especially in Norway in 1940.

Eric's own ship, the *Glorious*, along with its next-door neighbour, *Courageous*, were both to be converted into aircraft carriers, as has already been stated. *Furious* had already gone through some sort of conversion, being listed here as 'aircraft vessel'. Suffice it to say that all these three ships, as aircraft carriers, did not survive long into the war. *Hermes* and *Ark Royal,* which were the first purpose-built aircraft carriers, lasted longer.

Eric tells how they had been anchored in their usual billet off Burntisland, where they had been *all the summer pretty well without a break*. The King came round in the destroyer *Oak*, and passed them soon after 11 a.m. Anchored with them were *Minotaur*, *Vindictive* and *Argus*. The last two ships are described by him as 'flying ships'. Eric describes his own ship, *Glorious*, as being particularly large. On the chart it is listed as a cruiser. However, there does seem to be some element of doubt about it because in the naval lists at this time it does not give any category. *As our ship is so big we can only man one side at a time, so when he* [the King] *came back the other side we had to rush over and man the other side!*

On the Thursday morning, 21 November, at 2.45 a.m. they put to sea and proceeded towards May Island. *I had the morning watch so was up on the compass platform at 4.00 a.m. We expected to meet the German Fleet any time after 8.00 a.m.* He was relieved soon after in order to get breakfast before they closed for action stations

as we weren't going to take any risks of foul play. The German Fleet was sighted about 8.00 a.m. and we went to Action Stations about 9.00 a.m. In the fore-turret, my station, we had everything in readiness. The guns were all ready for loading and the turret was free to train. About 9.30 a.m. it was reported that the German Battle Cruisers were in sight and we saw them, five in number, following astern of one of our Light Cruisers ['Cardiff']. Their guns were all trained fore and aft, and as soon as I saw that they did not look as though they were going to give us any trouble, I came out and watched them from the top of the turret. Astern of the Battle Cruisers came four Battleships of the Kaiser Class and then the 'Bayern' with her 15 inch guns, and astern of her four Battleships of the Konig Class. [According to the chart, 'Bayern' came after the 'Prinzregent Leopold'.] You can imagine how interesting it was to try and pick out the different classes from the silhouettes which we had so often studied during the last few years.

Behind the battleships came another British light cruiser, the *Phaeton*, and then astern of her seven German light cruisers. These were followed by the German destroyers. There were *forty-nine all told, as one had been lost on the way over by striking a mine, but they have been told to send another one over to replace it.* Destroyers are not included on the chart apart from a few British ones acting as escorts.

The weather was misty, but even so clearer than it had been for several days past. On the way back Eric's squadron had passed the German Fleet anchored below the island of Inchkeith. *It was about 3.15 p.m. and the sun was beginning to set behind them and I think it was a sight never to be forgotten. The mighty German High Seas Fleet surrounded by British Battleships.* Then, finally, there was Admiral Beatty's much remembered signal to the German Admiral that at sunset the German flags were to be hauled down and not to be re-hoisted without permission. Their ships were to remain there for 48 hours in order to be thoroughly inspected to see that all the terms of the Armistice had been carried out, and then they would be interned in Scapa Flow.

It is interesting to compare Eric's reaction to this event with that of Sub Lieutenant Hyde C. Burton, RN, who recorded these events, also in a letter to his mother. His ship was the battleship *Neptune*. This is included in *The Imperial War Museum Book of the First World War Part VIII, The Last Act at Sea*, by Malcolm Brown. While Eric's reaction is almost one of amazement that the German Fleet had surrendered, Hyde Burton is also amazed, but his amazement is centred round the humiliation of the event for the Germans: *I cannot understand how they could possibly have surrendered so ignominiously without making a show.* However, his motives do seem a little mixed because he expresses sorrow for *their utter defeat,* almost immediately after he talks about the disappointment of being *done out of our scrap.* In the same chapter of the book, Ernest Fox, a chief steward who saw the whole thing from the *Royal Oak*, says: *To see such magnificent ships surrender to another fleet was pitiful really. What would have happened had Britain been in the same position? Would we have surrendered? I don't think so.*

Malcolm Brown quotes Admiral Beatty as finding something

'pitiable' about the surrender but his general attitude seems to have been one of bluff contempt.

It was a pitiable sight, in fact I should say it was a horrible sight to see those great ships . . . expecting them to have the same courage that we expect from men whose work lies in great waters. We did expect them to do something for the honour of their country. They are now going to be taken away and placed under the guardianship of the Grand Fleet at Scapa . . . They have nothing to look forward to except degradation.

However, six months later is was to be the German Fleet which had the last word when it scuttled itself in Scapa Flow. It was a pity that Admiral Beatty could not have shown a greater spirit of generosity in his comments.

For Eric, after the day's events, there was a thanksgiving service – *One of the most impressive I have ever attended. Our work now in the Grand Fleet is nearly over and it is difficult to realise, as it has come so suddenly.* Later, he worked it out that *on that day, 21st November, the Grand Fleet consisted of over eighty-one capital ships and two hundred Destroyers, so perhaps the Germans were wise to give up their Fleet.*

The letter finishes with a reference to his sister Aline, who appears to have succumbed to the extremely serious bout of influenza which ravaged the country at the end of the war in 1918, with such effect that people have even compared its depredations with war casualties at the time. Having thanked his mother for her letter he then says he is most anxious to hear about Aline, adding that *it isn't the influenza that is so dangerous, but the pneumonia which you are so liable to get afterwards.* Then there is an instruction about taking great care and keeping her in bed until all possible danger is past. I think he was rather better at giving this sort of advice than he would have been in following it himself if it had been necessary!

Lastly there is mention of Shedden, his brother, and Alec, his brother-in-law, both serving on the Western Front, whom he supposes will be taking part in the Army of Occupation.

The next letter was only three days later. He was anxious

whether his mother had received his letter of 22 November about the German surrender. *I should like the letter kept for future reference*. It certainly was kept, but, after his mother died in 1934 and his father in 1944, all his correspondence came back to him and was with his own possessions when he died in 1982. In this second letter he enclosed three photographs of the *Courageous*, the sister ship of his own *Glorious*. The photographs apparently demonstrated, along with his own explanation, how a two-seater plane was launched from the top of a gun turret. One of Eric's duties was to give the orders for 'slipping' the machine, which ran down a 40–foot platform placed on top of the turret, 'into the air'. He rightly states that this was a responsible job as *you have the lives of two men in your hands, and if a mistake is made they would be killed*. It was rather a matter of getting the right wind speed, between 25 and 30 mph, and training the turret into the wind. The aeroplane concerned was a reconnaissance aircraft, carrying enough fuel to remain in the air for about four hours, after which it would come down in the water near a destroyer and (one hopes very much) the two airmen would be picked up. The machine would float for about half an hour and then sink – *you can see that the flying officers have a pretty risky time of it*. That seems to be putting it mildly! He then explains how they recently had a fatal accident because the wind speed had been too great for the machine's power. It had just fallen sideways off the turret, crashed on the ship's side and into the water, and the pilot was killed. On this occasion Eric was not in charge of the 'flying off'.

The rest of the letter describes how the old liner *Campania* had sunk three weeks before this. On the night of a tremendous gale the *Campania* had dragged her anchor and been swept onto the bows of the *Royal Oak*. Then both ships were dragged onto the *Glorious*, whose captain eventually got his ship clear. In the end the *Campania* went down but everyone was saved. *Curiously enough the Captain of the 'Campania' was our old commander in the 'Nottingham' and in this ship [Glorious] until about three months ago*, i.e. Captain Miller. The *Campania* had been used as an 'aeroplane ship'.

The letter finishes with the hope that Aline is better and that there is no likelihood of complications regarding her influenza.

So Eric's war ended. One final observation is that during almost the entire war he never saw promotion. In the normal course of events in war, promotion occurs because of vacancies arising because people are killed. Obviously, too, it is often a matter of being in the right place at the right time. However, this also demonstrates how in this war in particular, one's chances of survival at sea were infinitely greater than they were on land.

12

Early in 1919 Eric joined HMS *Southampton*, another light cruiser and sister ship of the *Northampton*, sunk in 1916. However, this was only temporary because with effect from 7 April 1919 he was at HMS *Egmont* in Malta. He wrote home to his mother on 10 May stating he was very comfortable and *as far as I can see my duties will not be very onerous. I am 1st Lieutenant of an enormous fort called St Angelo. I have a beautiful big cabin and it has French windows opening on to a balcony which has a magnificent view looking out on to the entrance to the harbour here.* He was in charge of all the Maltese ratings and their accommodation at St Angelo. This had its problems as *they don't understand a word of English*, and he had to give his orders through a Maltese CPO. Anyhow, he found the Maltese very willing and explains how his own Maltese servant did everything for him most efficiently. It certainly sounds like the peace-time navy. *He helps me with my chair and he has a newspaper propped in front of me ready to read, so you can tell how comfortable I am.* All told, he found it an excellent place and much better than being at home.

Then there is an interesting remark, evidence of a changing world: *There are no Socialists here and you are treated with proper respect.* He goes on to enthuse about the climate. Altogether he seems to have found himself a good billet. He admits that the place *will spoil me for home waters.* However, as events were to show, it was not quite so soft and easy as he had anticipated. Another letter, again to his mother, followed in a fortnight's time on 24 May. Everything was going well. Apart from going into summer uniform and avoiding mosquitoes, there was little news and the letter is accordingly fairly brief. Enclosing some photographs, he comments that the fort, St Angelo, was built by Arabs in AD 720.

When he writes again about a week later on 2 June, it is to his father. Much of the content is social – e.g. a grand dinner given at the Maltese Club in Valetta, and the visit of the World Billiards Champion, who gave an exhibition game at the Maltese Club – and he also gives quite a detailed account of his visit to the Cathedral of St John, which contains the tombs of many of the Knights of Malta. He speaks with enthusiasm of all the cathedral's chapels and what he learned from them. Apparently he developed quite an interest in the history of the island.

However, in this letter he talks rather less about the privileges of his position and more about the responsibilities. *I find the work here is a pretty big responsibility as there is so much to be done in a large establishment like this. I now have to look after the recruitment of Maltese men to take the place of Englishmen who are going home to be demobilised. I think I am doing pretty well so far!*

His final comment in this letter is interesting: *We seem very much at war out here as we keep sending men and ships from here to Constantinople and the Black Sea. Today a Russian Destroyer was towed in here.* At this stage the allied treaty with Turkey had been by no means finalised and, in fact, it was not until August 1920 that the Treaty of Sèvres was concluded. In the meantime the Allied fleets and armies occupied Constantinople and the Straits. As the Russian Civil War was then raging, this could have indirectly had some bearing on the Russian destroyer being towed into Valetta.

When he writes again on 15 June to his mother, they have their own trouble in Malta. *I think this will have to be a very long letter as I have so much to write about.* The letter started peacefully enough with an account of a motor drive to Civita Vecchia, the ancient capital of the island, then to St Paul's Bay, returning by another route which took in an interesting church *with an enormous dome 204 feet high.* On their return to Valetta at 5.30 p.m. they noticed that the Strada Reale was very crowded, but as they knew there was going to be a big labour meeting that day they did not think much of it, and so returned to their club.

However, something was obviously wrong. The excitement outside now became more intense with the crowd getting even bigger. Eric thought it wise to return to *Egmont*, where he arrived safely at 6.30 p.m. He had just got to his room when the Commander came in and said, 'Look here, Number One, there is a riot on the shore and we have to land every available man.'

He collected the men and armed them with rifles and ammunition. By this time men were arriving from other ships in the harbour, all armed. When they mustered at Fort Angelo they were over 400. The marines were sent ashore at once to the Customs House. The rest of them waited on the jetty until midnight, and as nothing had happened they dispersed for the night. The marines returned later, *not having accomplished anything though the situation was pretty ugly*. It appeared that the mob had first attacked the university, breaking all the windows, and then burning all the books. The military had been called out and there had been casualties among the rioters. Eric heard from several officers who came off at 7.30 a.m. that they had had to run the gauntlet, and one captain had his face cut open. There had been cries of 'Down with the British.' All that had taken place on the Saturday. On Sunday everything had proceeded as usual until at 10.15 a.m. there was another alarm. There was rioting in Valetta and orders were given to land every man. Once more Eric assembled his men and armed them; he himself was armed with sword and revolver. *I was given charge of a hundred men and I divided them up into two companies putting a Warrant Officer in charge of each, myself in general charge.* His two companies and the marines landed on the Customs House jetty, where there were also 40 men with one Lewis gun, from the *Stuart*. They remained on the jetty all day, *going across and getting our meals in watches*.

They could not tell what was going on except from telephone messages, but it did seem rather serious. Then they received a message to say that their *beautiful Union Club was being attacked and to send help at once or the mob would get in.* The marines were sent up at the double to see what was happening. No sooner had they set off than orders were received to recall them. Although it was too late, the marines returned of their own accord shortly afterwards. They reported that the Strada Reale was packed with people and they had to fix bayonets and charge down the street to the Union Club with *all the people scurrying away like rabbits*. The Maltese then informed them that everything was quite all right and they must return, which, of course, they did. *We heard afterwards that everything was far from alright and the position was really serious*. Stones were being thrown in at windows and they were trying to break down the doors. One assumes that all this was taking place at the Union Club.

> *The waiters had all fled and there were about eight officers imprisoned and unarmed inside. One Engineer Commander who tried to get in to get away from the mob could not get them to open the doors and whilst he was beating on the doors he was attacked. He put up a good fight for it before they got him down and started to kick his body and otherwise maltreat him. Luckily someone observed him from the Club and they got him inside very much cut about and bruised; and the Maltese police, the Blighters, had told us everything was alright! There we were, all waiting and the Governor would not let us go and help.*

They then heard that they were attacking a house belonging to a wealthy Maltese opposite the opera house, and still they received no orders to move. Eventually, at 7.30 p.m. the orders came. The marines led the way, followed by Eric's two companies, the *Stuart's* men bringing up the rear. They proceeded by the Victoria Gate up the San Giovanni steps and into the Strada Mercanti, and halted at the Castille. Everything was quiet there but there was noise from the Strada Reale. They were met there by Captain Trewby, the captain of *Egmont*, who told them that looting was going on and they must clear the streets *if possible without bloodshed*. It was now nearly dark. *We fixed bayonets and loaded rifles. This completed, we charged down a side street and into the Opera Square, I with my sword drawn. It is difficult for me to describe what the clearing of the crowd was really like, but it was something I have never witnessed before!*

When they came upon them quite unawares, the rioters fled

before them *like rabbits*. There was a vast roar, several shots were fired and something was thrown at them, but nobody appeared to be hit. They took about half a minute to clear the place and then turned their attention to the house being looted. Having drawn cordons all across the entrances to the square, as the looters came out of the side door of the house they endeavoured to arrest them, but a good many got away by running down the street the other way. It was dangerous to approach too near the house as they were throwing things down on top of them. *Also there was a man on a bridge nearby, firing at us with a Browning revolver, but we managed to shoot him. Our men were now getting rather excited and it was difficult to restrain them from shooting, but this we did as much as possible. Some of the men, before they were captured, got badly stabbed with bayonets.* Eric is somewhat dismissive of the Maltese militia, who were standing in the background by the railway station, doing nothing. *They made no attempt to stop the looting and the officers seemed quite useless and helpless.*

The looters remaining in the house now seemed reluctant to come out and so Eric accompanied some of his men inside. The looters had jammed a table in the doorway to prevent an easy entrance, so the men had to climb over this in order to enter. Eric was obviously impressed by the house itself. *I have never seen such a magnificent house. The Ritz Hotel was not in it!* However, the contents were not exactly Ritz-like. *Everything in the house was smashed, carpets, beds, tables and chairs, all smashed and thrown about anyhow. I have never seen such a mess or such colossal destruction, more like a chateau in France during the war.* He first went down to the cellar, where there was nothing apart from broken bottles of wine. Upstairs he found a bathroom with all the taps running, which he turned off. Eventually, after exploring and finding nothing that was not smashed, apart from small bundles of loot dropped by the looters in their hurry, he discovered some men up a backstairs in an attic. The door was locked, so they broke it open with a rifle and caught about 24 looters. *These we drove before us at the end of bayonets.*

Unfortunately, he lost his way and had the humiliation of asking the prisoners to show him how to get out. *They were a miserable lot and as soon as they found out they weren't going to*

71

be killed on the spot they poured blessings down on my head which I resented.

When they came out into the street and went down to the picket house, the excitement had died down. All the prisoners were collected, the badly wounded taken to hospital, and the rest marched off to the Castille, where the military took them over. There were 38 in all.

Eric does not seem to have a very high opinion of the army. *The curious part about the whole rising was that the military seemed to be doing nothing at all and were leaving it entirely to the Navy.* I suppose that for a land-based operation it did seem curious.

By now armed sailors were parading the streets and clearing everyone out.

I now took a well earned rest by sitting on the steps of the Opera House and surveying the scene of destruction. The street was littered with debris that had been thrown out of the windows. There were rolls and rolls of pianola records lying all over the place and a pianola half way out of a window, which they were about to throw out when we disturbed them. It was now about 10.00 p.m., and as I had had nothing since tea, I was feeling rather peckish, so a few of us went round to the Great Britain Hotel close by, and got a welcome drink and some sandwiches, and here I learnt some of the experiences of other people.

Eric then marched his men back to the Customs House, where they embarked for the fort, arriving back just before midnight after *one of the most eventful days of my life.* Everything was now quiet in Valetta. Eric heard later that the owner of the 'magnificent house', with his wife and children, had hidden in the farthest part of the cellars which Eric had visited without finding anyone. *It is a good thing that the looters did not find them or they would have been murdered.*

The following day, Monday, he was sent off in charge of a hundred men with two warrant officers, in a drifter, to Marsa, right up at the end of the harbour. He had been given orders to protect the flour mills there and also the gasworks and the

72

petroleum tanks. They landed at about 8.15 a.m. and approached St Andrew's Mill. As they came near, Eric perceived that looting was in full swing. He immediately gave orders for the men to charge with fixed bayonets. The looters, as soon as they saw them coming, started *flying off in all directions*, and by the time the sailors came up, most of the looters had cleared out.

So great was their hurry to get away that they dropped everything and ran. Sacks of flour and semolina were strewn all over the road, and as the carts dashed along the road sacks of flour kept tumbling off into the road, which was most amusing to watch. Eventually they scattered into the fields and got away in the long grass.

Soon after this Eric found a telephone and got in touch with the Castille, and as a result an armed steamboat came down to take off the prisoners. There were only two! He still had trouble with the crowds who kept assembling down at the mills. His men were continually having to disperse them with bayonets, and sometimes firing shots over their heads, but towards midday things began to quieten down. Captain Trewby came down in a motor to inspect the place and asked Eric if he needed reinforcements. Having told him that he did not, he then thought better of it and asked for a further 100 men, so as to be on the safe side. Eventually 120 came, with a lieutenant commander, to whom Eric now handed over his command. The only other event with which he was involved was the funeral procession of one of the men who had been shot during the disturbances on Saturday. However, everything passed off quietly and they had no further trouble. *Evidently they are getting frightened at our show of force.*

They remained at the Marsa until 11.30 p.m. Eric returned to the fort at 12.30 a.m. and the following day took things easy. Patrols continued to be sent ashore, the next day in particular because the new Governor, Sir Henry Plumer, was due to arrive from Marseilles. However, despite all leave being stopped, it seemed that the trouble was over. Four days later the court martial for the prisoners took place. *They had picked out the worst characters among the prisoners for trial, and a more villainous lot I have never seen, with typical criminal faces.* All RN personnel made statements about what had occurred. *I hope they* [the prisoners] *will get severe sentences.* He finishes his letter with the request, *Please keep this letter as I think it will make interesting reading in later years.*

This letter is a long one, over 15 pages. It is followed by a much shorter one to his mother a week later, in which he hopes his previous letter telling about the riots has been received. As it happened it had not arrived, even by the next week. Anyhow, it was very much back to normal, according to this second letter. The main topic is how hot the weather was becoming and the wearing of semi-tropical kit including a sun helmet. He bathed a lot, early in the morning at 7.30 a.m. *Figs are now in full swing.* (A strange metaphor!)

The letter continues the following day, 23 June, with thanks for a letter he had just received from home. He is amused because it mentions the Malta Riots, which one assumes his parents have read about in the newspaper, and hopes that they did not disturb him at all.

The picture is not quite so idyllic as in the first part of the letter. The Commander had gone sick, so *I am running the place entirely on my own.* There had been an accident the previous night when a man fell a distance of 50 feet and was killed. Eric had had to make out a report and arrange for an inquest and a funeral. He was feeling his responsibilities very much. *I find I have to be a sort of mine of information here as everybody is sent to 'Egmont' if they don't know what to do, and they all come to see me as First Lieutenant.* On that note he ends.

A week later Eric writes again and one cannot help feeling he is doing so with a certain amount of indignation. *I see you have not received my long letter telling you about the riots. You say you did not see the Navy mentioned so you thought they were not concerned, but it was quite the other way round, and the Navy did the whole thing, the military and the police doing practically nothing.* One can well understand his indignation. The rest of the letter is fairly routine although it is interesting to note he mentions that *yesterday we officially celebrated the signing of the Peace and fired a salute of 101 guns and spliced the mainbrace i.e. extra tot of rum all round.*

Eric final letter in this series is dated 6 July 1919. He mentions the final courts martial regarding the prisoners from the riots. Reference to the war is still evident with a special thanksgiving service in St Paul's Cathedral, Valetta. There is talk too of demobilisation. Finally there is an interesting comment about a letter he had received from a fellow in Belgrade. *He tells us that Admiral Trowbridge is looked upon as the uncrowned king of Serbia, and they won't let him go, and nothing is being done without consulting him.*

Admiral Trowbridge had been involved with Balkan affairs for some time. In 1915 he was head of the British Naval Mission to Serbia, and then Admiral Commander on the Danube in 1918. He was the great-grandson of a famous captain who had fought under Nelson at the Battle of the Nile in 1798.

13

At this point my uncle's correspondence ends and I can only piece together from the Navy Lists and various other documents which he preserved, the remainder of his career in the Royal Navy.

He stayed in Malta until April 1921. For May and June of that year he does not appear to have had a ship, so possibly he was on a course, although with effect from 18 June he appears in the list as Flag-Lieutenant. Then in July he is with HMS *Hercules*, a battleship, with the Reserve Fleet at Rosyth, commanded by his old friend Millar, now Rear Admiral. In August he is with HMS *New Zealand*, a battle cruiser, and in November with HMS *Lion* in the same station and under the same overall command. He remained at Rosyth until May 1922, when he went off to Portsmouth on an observer's course.

On 30 August he received his promotion to Lieutenant Commander, but was not listed again until February 1923, when he joined the battleship HMS *Queen Elizabeth* under the C.-in-C. Atlantic Fleet, Admiral De Roebeck. In January 1924 he joined the aircraft carrier HMS *Argus*, being listed as 'additional', for observer duties. Fortunately he kept a photographic record of the period of his life from 1924 to 1928. There are photographs of the quarter deck of HMS *Argus*, a seaplane and the wreckage in the water of another seaplane. Then there are numerous photographs of individual ships of the fleet, and indeed the fleet itself in Arosa Bay, all taken in March and April 1924. In October he was transferred to another aircraft carrier, the *Hermes*. I am uncertain just how many *Hermes* aircraft carriers there have been. The 1924 *Hermes* was, I believe, the first one to be built as an aircraft carrier and was not a converted battleship. It certainly looks a very handsome ship all dressed out for the Spithead Review of 1924.

Eric was with HMS *Hermes* under Captain Stopford until April 1925, when he left to go on a flying course at Netheravon in Wiltshire which lasted until the end of June. He then returned to *Hermes*, and there is a photograph dated July 1925 of the ship leaving Malta for China.

After Port Said and Aden, the next port of call was in Ceylon (Sri Lanka). Among the interesting photographs taken in Trincomali, is one entitled 'Group at Rest House' (seven officers out of uniform but wearing topees). Then it is on to Singapore and finally Hong Kong.

Eric had now come to what was always known as 'The China Station'. *Hermes* seems to have been out on the China Station from the end of 1925 for the better part of two years. During that time the ship had three captains, Stopford, Talbot, and Elliott. Eric's time at the RAF Training School at Netheravon seems to have borne fruit and there is good photography of His Excellency the Governor of Hong Kong flying round the New Territories in a Fairy III seaplane, the crew of the aircraft being Flight Lieutenant Moulton Barrett, RAF (pilot), Lieutenant Commander Woodruff, RN (observer), and HE the Governor (passenger).

Included among the photographs are many of British North Borneo or, as it is now, Sabah, and Labuan, which seems to be in Brunei. Although there are photographs of Hong Kong dated 1925, 1926 and 1927, the indication is that *Hermes* returned to Malta during this period. His photographic record of European locations indicates either service in the Mediterranean or periods of leave, e.g. Argostoli in Greece, Trieste, Innsbruck and Venice. Then it is back to Hong Kong.

The *Hermes* stayed out on the China Station until the summer of 1927, according to the photographs, and by October he, and most probably *Hermes*, were on the way home.

In January 1928 Eric joined HMS *Furious*, another aircraft carrier, but *An ugly looking beast after HMS Hermes* – being, like HMS *Glorious*, a converted battleship. He was with *Furious* from January until June 1928, and during this short period had three different captains. There is one interesting photograph of three officers on the flight deck of HMS *Furious*, one of whom is the Admiral of the Fleet, Lord Jellicoe. The spring cruise of the *Furious* seems to have taken Eric to Gibraltar, but in June they were back in Scapa Flow, and there is a photograph of the scuttled *Hindenburg* just protruding above the waterline.

For 13 months after leaving HMS *Furious* in July 1928, Eric was *with HMS Vivid for HMS Glorious* – whatever that means! From September to December 1929 he was employed rewriting *Admiralty Publication OU538 – Annual Air Gunnery and Bombing Practices to be carried out by the Fleet Air Arm*. Then from January 1930 until January 1932 he appears to have been on loan to the RAF at their base at Gosport. From January 1932 to March 1933 he was on HMS *Eagle*, another aircraft carrier, employed on observer duties *in an advisory capacity whilst ship refitting*. Finally from June 1933 to June 1934 he was on HMS *Calypso*, a 4180-ton cruiser of the Reserve Fleet at Devonport.

By now he was coming up for retirement. In December 1934 he would have been 42 years old, which one assumes was the age for retirement of those of the rank of Lieutenant Commander. He retired with the rank of Commander, but in the event, because of the outbreak of World War II in September 1939, he was only to be 'out' for less than five years.

So, in December 1934 Eric went onto the Retired/Reserve List of Officers. There is little information I can find about this period of his life. He lived at the family home, which was now in Oakwood Avenue, Beckenham, Kent. His father was there, aged 84 but reasonably active, not having as yet taken to his bed. As a very small boy myself, I can recall being taken there and not really being able to distinguish between the two men, my grandfather of 84 and my uncle of 42, unless I saw them both together – but then to the very young everybody seems much the same age after they are about 20!

As was to be expected, Eric took a job, but what this was I do not know. There is a copy of a letter to the Mercantile Marine Department of the Board of Trade, applying for the *Unestablished post of Inspector, East Anglian Division, HM Coastguards* dated 9 March 1936, and the only other letter of any kind is one signed 'Louis Mountbatten' and dated 1 October

1938, accepting Eric's resignation of the Secretaryship of the Royal Naval Flying Club.

Eric's name next appears in the Navy List of October 1940 under HMS *Victory*, as Staff Officer (Operations), taking effect from 1 April 1940. This suggests that as a retired reservist he was not recalled until at least seven months after the outbreak of war, which seems to make reasonable sense. He seems to have been based at Portsmouth.

That period appears to have lasted until 30 September 1942 because there is a certificate signed by a Commodore (signature illegible) acting on behalf of the Admiral in Chief, Portsmouth, stating that he has served as Staff Officer, Home Defence. There is a gap here because the next certificate dates from 9 August 1943 to 7 December 1943. However, his name does appear in the Navy List for December 1942, again as Staff Officer, but this time 'Local Defence', and again under HMS *Victory*.

In the list of 1943 his name is under HMS *Shrike*, and the certificate taking effect from 9 August 1943 is signed by the Captain, HMS *Shrike*. There is a photograph dated 7 November 1941 of Eric with three other officers on board MVF *Massabielle for trials of arming 'R' mine torts with dummy mines*. He describes himself as *Cmdr. Woodruff. C.-in-C. Office Ports*. From HMS *Shrike* he was transferred to HMS *Flora* (Parent Ship) Invergordon on 1 January 1944. This is evidenced both by the Navy List and by a certificate signed by the Captain of HMS *Flora*. This lasted until 9 October 1944.

His final posting was to HMS *Pyramus* (Parent Ship) Kirkwall, which effectively meant that he was Commanding Officer and RNO at Kirkwall, in the Orkneys. This took effect, according to the Navy List, from 11 October 1944 (although his certificate only takes effect from 1 March 1945). He remained on the Navy List until October 1945.

This was the period of my uncle's service in World War II, about which I recall hearing most and, certainly, until I checked up on the Navy Lists, I had always assumed it was considerably longer. For Christmas 1944 our family enjoyed a turkey sent down from the Orkneys, as did two other branches of the family. We regarded ourselves as fortunate to have a turkey. Rationing and everything that went with it was at its worst at that time. This gift created amongst the family what was probably a myth, that in the Orkneys rationing meant very little, and that Uncle Eric, billeted as he was in the Kirkwall Hotel, was living off the fat of the land. From this grew a further myth, that he sat out the war in the Orkneys in a really cushy billet. The facts show this to be something of an exaggeration. Certainly rationing may have meant less in the Orkneys than it did in the cities of the UK, but the point is that Eric would have only enjoyed this for the last seven months of the war.

Eric's service came to an end in July 1945. He returned to the family home at Beckenham in August and I can recall meeting up with him at tea in the garden there. He had arrived about an hour previously and was still in uniform, but it was to be the final occasion. He would have been 53 years old.

Shortly after this Eric purchased a property at Netherbury in Dorset, which now became the rather smaller Woodruff home. His younger sister, May, lived there with him, along with his brother Shedden and his niece Phyllis when they returned from Australia in 1948. This household split up in 1959. For a short period Eric lived in private hotels in Bridport and Shaftesbury, but by 1962 he was ensconced within the community at Pythouse, a retirement home near Tisbury in Wiltshire. He lived there long enough to celebrate his ninetieth birthday in December 1981. As a result of a bad fall at Pythouse on 1 July 1982, he was transferred to hospital in Salisbury, and from there to a nursing home where he died on 12 August 1982. The funeral was held at Tisbury Parish Church on 18 August, and in accordance with his will his remains were interred at Chislehurst cemetery next to his mother's grave.

APPENDICES

July 23rd	During the forenoon a court of inquiry was held on board because the gun mountings of the ship were defective. Hands scrub & wash clothes.
July 24th	Left Southend at 6.30 a.m. & proceeded to Dover, arriving there at noon. During the afternoon H.M.S. Bonaventure & 6 submarines came in.
July 25th	At 5.30 a.m. Monsieur Bleriot crossed the channel in his monoplane. Ordinary routine carried out.
July 26th	At 9.0 a.m. left harbour for carrying out rate of change & plotting exercises but owing to the state of the sea returned to harbour at 11.30 a.m.
July 27th	Left harbour at 9.0 a.m. & carried out plotting & turning exercises. At 6.0 P.M. Mr Latham failed to cross channel for 2nd time in his aeroplane. The picket boat was sent out to assist but that of the Russell arrived there first.
July 28th	At 9.0 a.m. left harbour with the Formidable & carried out plotting exercises returned during afternoon. At 7.30 left Dover for Cowes.
July 29th	After divisions rehearsed "Cheer ship". Entered Solent and anchored off Cowes at 1.0 P.M.

A page of Eric's Midshipman's Journal for 1909 which includes mention of Bleriot's channel flight.

H.M.S. NOTTINGHAM,
FIRST FLEET.

Immingham
July 3rd 1914.

Dear Father

Thank you so very much indeed for the cheques which I received all safely.

We arrived here on Wednesday evening from Kiel for the Nottingham festivities as this is the nearest port which we can get to Nottingham. We left Kiel at 7.30 on Tuesday morning and came through the Kiel Canal which was most interesting + I managed to get a couple of photographs. We entered the canal at 8.0 in the morning and did not get out until 4.0 in the afternoon. All day we were passing through pretty scenery of woods and fields and farm houses it seemed so funny + out of place with the

Extracts from Eric's letter to his father, casually mentioning the assassination of the Austrian Archduke.

ship which one always associated with the sea.
We had to strike our topmasts in order to get under
the bridges.
All the festivities arranged for on Sunday and Ma-
-day at Kiel were put off owing to the assassination
of the Crown Prince of Austria so we had a welcome
rest on those two days. Phyllis Tipping never came
to tea on Monday which was a pity as we had a
lot of German ladies on board for tea...
Yesterday we took in 400 tons of coal which was
tedious work and took us 12 hours owing to our
having to hoist it in with our own winches on board.
Tomorrow, Saturday, most of us are going up to
Nottingham to a luncheon and the silver plate
will be presented to us. One of the pieces is a
silver model of the 1st Nottingham and ought
to make an imposing table centre. There are also
other things such as Gunnery shields etc.
On Monday we are entertaining 25 members of
the Nottingham Navy League to lunch and also
300 people are coming to tea and see over the
ship. As they arrive in a special train at 1·0 p·m

and don't leave till 6.0 p.m we shall have our work cut out to entertain them for 5 hours. And as we don't know one of them I should not be at all surprised if we don't get a lot of local people in

as well who have been self invited.

We leave for Portland on Tuesday night and then we go to Spithead for the Reviews. We arrive at Spithead at 6.0 p.m on Thursday and leave on Monday so I may be able to get home one of those days to see you. I hear on good authority that we shall be able to have some guests on board for the Review if as it will be a good opportunity for some to come & see the ship. But more details of this later on.

Please could you send me my photos which I left at home the ones taken by Russell I mean as I have promised one to Brookes.

We had a bad thunderstorm on our arrival here which was not a very good welcome back to England & to-day it is pouring with rain, I hope it will be fine for our Nottingham trip.

We had no rough weather at all on our

trip to Kiel both going & returning beyond the fog the
weather was good so the papers were quite wrong about
that. On our arrival at Kiel the night before
we went into the harbour we had a thunderstorm
& so perhaps they meant that.
I shall not be getting leave so early as July 13th
except for the Reviews I think.
Please thank Mother & Marjory for their letters.
            Your loving Son.
                Eric.

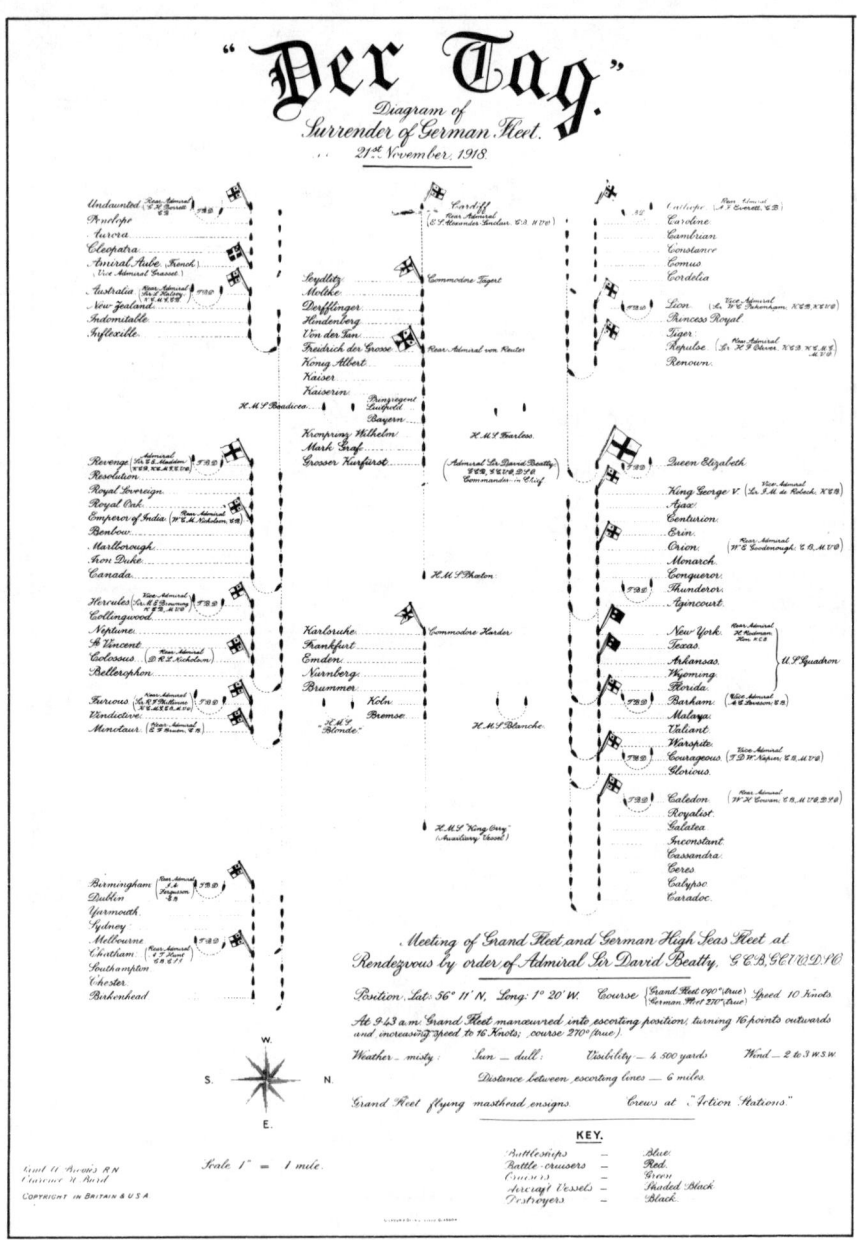

Copy from Official Battle Plan for surrender of German Fleet. 21st November 1918.

INDEX